Back in the Saddle

Karen Templeton

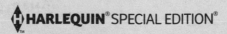

HARLEQUIN®SPECIAL EDITION®

Recycling programs
for this product may
not exist in your area.

ISBN-13: 978-0-373-65945-6

Back in the Saddle

Printed in U.S.A.

"You know what I'd really like to do right now?"

"I can't wait to hear this," he said, and her eyes twinkled.

"It's also been a while since a boy kissed me on a porch swing."

"You don't know what you're asking, Mallory."

"Actually, I do...oh." She huffed a sigh then said, "And here's where I should probably get off your lap and pretend like this never happened. If, you know, I could actually do that—"

"Oh, God, no, honey—" Zach grabbed her hand and pressed it to his chest. "That did not come out the way I meant it. Because trust me, I've been thinking about kissing you, too. For some time, actually."

Her lips curved. "You don't say."

"God's truth," he said, and she chuckled, low in her throat. "But...it's been a while since I've kissed a girl, too. On a porch swing or anyplace else. And I—"

"*Think far too much*, is how you want to finish that sentence," she murmured, then curved her hands around his jaw and brought their mouths together.

And in that instant, he knew *kissing* her would never be enough.

* * *

Dear Reader,

One thing I love about novel writing is how often the seeds for a character or story come from totally unexpected sources. In this case, a Facebook friend who uses a wheelchair suggested I write a heroine similar to her. I immediately embraced the idea...only to discover how very much I had to learn. And still do. But the research was beyond rewarding. And I'm more grateful than I can say for the opportunity to grow, not only as a writer, but into hopefully a more empathetic human being.

The same could be said for Zach and Mallory, each of whom helps the other stretch and grow, too, embracing possibilities where they'd thought none existed...proving that amazing things can happen in small towns and to anyone willing to let them happen.

I love these people, and I hope you will, too.

Blessings,

Karen

Karen Templeton is a recent inductee into the Romance Writers of America Hall of Fame. A three-time RITA® Award–winning author, she has written more than thirty novels for Harlequin. She lives in New Mexico with two hideously spoiled cats. She has raised five sons and lived to tell the tale, and she could not live without dark chocolate, mascara and Netflix.

Books by Karen Templeton

Harlequin Special Edition

Wed in the West

A Soldier's Promise
Husband Under Construction
Adding Up to Marriage
Welcome Home, Cowboy
A Marriage-Minded Man
Reining in the Rancher
A Mother's Wish

Jersey Boys

Meant-to-Be Mom
Santa's Playbook
More Than She Expected
The Real Mr. Right

Summer Sisters

The Marriage Campaign
A Gift for All Seasons
The Doctor's Do-Over

The Fortunes of Texas: Whirlwind Romance

Fortune's Cinderella

Visit the Author Profile page at Harlequin.com for more titles.

To Jewel Kats
Who planted the seed.
Thanks, sweetie.

To Kari Lynn Dell
Who answered my horse/ranching/rodeo questions
with her usual aplomb, good humor and patience.
If I goofed, that's my fault,
not hers.

Chapter One

"So I gather you know a fair amount about horses?"

With an actual sigh, the getting-up-there Boston terrier slid down on the exam table in front of Zach Talbot and promptly went to sleep. *This might take a while, wake me when she's done.*

She being the auburn-haired Texan female of indeterminate age who'd brought the dog into Zach's clinic three times in the two weeks since she—and her daughter, she'd mentioned more than once—had moved into the old Hufsteter place a ways out of town. Completely renovated, she'd said. Beautiful house. Reminded her of home.

Not that Zach minded chatter, as a general rule. At least it kept him from curling up in a ball inside his own head. However, since he'd yet to find anything really wrong with the little dog, other than a general slowing down due to old age, he was guessing Dorelle Keyes had ulterior motives. Motives that Zach strongly suspected had something to do with this hitherto unseen daughter.

One hooded doggy lid briefly fluttered open as if to say *You got it, buddy*, before drifting closed again, and Zach met Dorelle's sharp—oh, *so* sharp—green gaze.

"As part of my practice, sure." After gently rubbing the dog between the ears—which got a soft groan—Zach scribbled down a couple notes for Shantelle at the front desk to add to Edgar's chart, then glanced back at Dorelle. Remembered to smile. "Why?"

"Oh. Well, Mallory—" the daughter "—is thinking about buying a horse for her boy. She's..." Dorelle glanced around, then practically mouthed, "Divorced. And his daddy has custody at the moment—" Her red-lipsticked mouth slammed shut, as though she'd realized she'd gotten stuck in that narrow wedge between discretion and oversharing. "Anyway, when we noticed the stalls out back, that was the first thing we thought of, how much Landon might like to have a horse to ride when he's here. So I was wondering if maybe you knew of someone local who might be selling. And you strike me as somebody we could trust."

His mouth twitching, Zach adjusted his glasses. Although his own mother had always said he had one of those faces. However...

"Horses take a lot of work, ma'am—"

"And while I appreciate that your mama obviously taught you to respect your elders, trust me, no woman past a certain age actually likes to be *ma'amed*."

"My apologies, m—Mrs. Keyes."

"Apology accepted. And second... I know how much work horses take. Mallory's daddy was a rancher. So we know what to do. We just don't know who to see. Landon's eleven, by the way. Far as I'm concerned he should've had his own horse long ago. But life had other ideas."

Not for the first time, Zach got the feeling the woman was deliberately baiting him. As though she'd been given instructions not to blab about personal matters, but if someone asked…well. It would only be polite to answer, wouldn't it? Too bad for her, then, that Zach was sorely lacking in the curiosity department.

Although his own full plate probably had something to do with that. Not to mention a deeply entrenched sense of self-preservation that kept most locals from developing anything even remotely like real relationships with the outsiders who flitted in and out of Whispering Pines. The town was no Taos or Santa Fe, heaven knew, but northern New Mexico's clear, high desert air and pristine forests attracted its fair share of tourists and temporary residents. Especially during ski season, which was right around the corner. Granted, Zach could be as cordial to visitors as the next townie. Friendly, even. Especially since they often brought dogs, and he was the only vet in town. But get himself all tangled up in their lives?

Nope.

However, he smiled, focusing on the topic at hand. "Has your grandson said he'd like to ride?"

"Oh, my goodness, yes! He already has, actually. A few times out on a farm north of LA. Where we were living, you know."

Clearly Zach's cue—again—to ask what had brought them to Whispering Pines. Except he honestly didn't care.

Heidi would've, though. Because his wife hadn't known the meaning of *aloof*, embracing—often literally—everyone she saw as if they were best friends…

"Dr. Talbot? Is everything okay?"

With an actual jerk, Zach pulled his head out of his butt to meet Dorelle's gaze again. "Yeah, sorry…" He cleared his throat. Smiled. "Actually, my brother Josh is the foreman up at the Vista Encantada Ranch nearby—"

"Oh, yes, we passed it the other day when we were out

exploring. And your girl out front, she said your brother worked there. One of 'em, anyway."

Shantelle was young yet. She'd learn. "The Vista breeds champion quarter horses—which wouldn't be suitable for your needs—but from time to time they foster rescues, too. I seem to recall Josh saying something about an older gelding that'd been used to teach another rancher's kids to ride. I haven't seen the horse yet myself, but I'm sure you and your daughter would be welcome to go out and meet him."

Dorelle lit up as if someone'd flipped a switch. "That sounds perfect—"

"Dad-deeee!"

"Liam! No!"

The groggy little dog scrambled to his feet as, at the doorway to the exam room, Zach's older son grabbed his baby brother around his middle and yanked him back. "Sorry, Dad!" Jeremy grunted out around the redheaded, windmilling blur that was his three-year-old brother. "Grandma just dropped us off. Man, he's *fast*."

"So were you at that age," Zach said, then squatted in front of the pair, ruffling the little one's rust-colored curls. "I'm almost done, squirt. You wait outside with Jeremy, okay?"

But Liam threw himself so hard into Zach's arms he nearly knocked him over. He had no idea why the boy was so clingy—certainly a lot more than his older brother had been—but his hugs never failed to overwhelm Zach, with love and fear, both.

"Oh, don't send them out on my account," Dorelle said behind him, more gently than Zach would've expected. Yes, it was obvious she loved her daughter and grandson, but until that very moment he wouldn't've pegged her as a softy.

Even so, the boys knew the rules. Or at least Jeremy

did. To Liam, the concept of boundaries was still a little sketchy. So Zach detached himself from his son, then stood, trying for stern and failing miserably when those big, brown, getting-wetter-by-the-second eyes tilted up to his. So who was the softy now?

"Go with your brother," he said, steeling himself against those eyes, so much like his mama's Zach's own stung. "I won't be long. Why don't you think about what you want on your pizza while you're waiting?"

That did the trick. "Peesa?" Liam breathed, as if this was the most awesome suggestion ever.

"Yep. Now scoot."

After the boys left, Zach turned to find Dorelle watching him with one of *those* expressions, God help him.

"Neither one of 'em looks much like you."

"Truth," Zach said with a smile. "Although I was apparently as blond as Jeremy when I was his age."

"Which is?"

"Seven. Eight in a few months."

"And the little one?"

"Liam's three. He looks…" His throat caught. Damn. "He looks exactly like his mother."

"She must be one gorgeous creature."

Zach hesitated. "She was."

Dorelle sucked in a short breath. "I'm so sorry, Dr. Talbot. I didn't know."

Somehow, he doubted that. And it was the end of what had been a very long day, one that had left Zach so tired he could barely see straight. Meaning he found himself sorely lacking patience for whatever game this woman was playing.

"Really?"

The woman's eyes briefly widened before she released a short laugh. "I suppose I deserved that. Since I'm sure it'll come as no surprise that digging up information is a hobby of mine. Especially when I find myself in a new place and don't know anybody. But I swear to you, this is the first I'm hearing of it." She hesitated, then asked, "How long?"

Oh, what the hell. "Two years," he said, and she bit her lip, shaking her head. Then she pushed out a little breath.

"Folks tend to keep to themselves around here, don't they?"

"Pretty much." Although Shantelle's keeping it to *her*-self was nothing short of a miracle. Town nosy-body in training, that one.

"Yeah, it was the same way back in Springerville," Dorelle said. "There were absolutely no secrets between neighbors, but we had that circling the wagons thing *down*. And oh, dear Lord—" Her hand flew to her cheek. "You thought I had matchmaking on my mind, didn't you?"

Zach's mouth twitched. "I had wondered."

"Oh, dear boy, *no*. Not that you're not cute as a damn button, but I did think you were married. Not a whole lot to do around here. Just like Springerville. One learns," she said with a slight, almost regal, bow, "to make one's own entertainment. Although we really are looking for a horse. Talking about it, anyway. And I thought…"

Her eyes clouded. "My daughter Mallory's had some challenges of her own, this last little while. And this past year or so has been particularly hard on her. Not that she'd ever admit it, God knows. But if you ask me, she didn't buy a house out here in Nowhere, New Mexico—no offense—"

"None taken."

Dorelle nodded. "Anyway. She didn't buy that house except for one reason, and that was to hide."

"From?" Zach asked before he caught himself.

"Life. Her life, anyway. And I don't like it, not one little bit. Frankly it scares me, if you want to know the truth.

Like she's given up. And that's not like her." Her forehead puckered, the brunette looked down at the dog, who'd fallen back asleep. "So it occurred to me that getting her looking for a horse for Landon might… I don't know… break whatever this is that's got hold of her. Start to, anyway." Softly smiling, she met Zach's gaze again. "That's all I was about, I swear. I wasn't trying to fix you up."

"I appreciate that."

"Good." Dorelle reached over to snap a leash on the snoozing dog before lowering him to the floor, where he blinked, yawned, then sat back down, slightly shivering. "So you'll call me after you talk to your brother?"

"I'll ask him later. I don't have regular appointments on Saturday afternoons."

"Thank you so much."

However, as Zach herded his sons to their little blue-and-white house next door to the clinic, Dorelle's comments about her daughter swirled inside his overworked brain like afternoon dust in the sunshine.

Clearly he needed a hobby. Or at least a nap.

"Hi, Mom!"

Seeing her son's ginormous grin swallowing up the entire, if admittedly tiny, phone screen, Mallory Keyes felt her heart swell in her chest. If her precious boy was happy, then she was happy. Nothing else mattered.

Even though it killed her, not being able to touch him, smell him, every day. But Landon deserved a normal life. Well, as normal as the son of a shattered Hollywood power couple—God, she hated that term—could expect. And never let it be said that Mallory couldn't roll with the punches. Or set her own druthers aside in order to do what was best for her son.

And at least they had smartphones.

"Hey, baby," she said, steeling herself for that inevitable moment when the kid would groan and go, "Mom? Really? *Baby*?" He was eleven, after all. But that moment apparently was not today. Thank God. "How's it going?"

"Good." He shoved his hand through shaggy, blah-brown hair that softened what promised to be some pretty fine bone structure, heaven help them all. "Got an A on this project we had to do in science. *Without* Dad's help, you'll be happy to know."

"I am. What was the project on?"

"How mold grows. I had to keep samples in the fridge, it was so cool. Except Cristina kept trying to throw them out."

Their housekeeper. Sixty if she was a day, built like a warship, heart of gold. "Sounds about right. She making you keep your room clean?"

"You better believe it," Mallory heard in the background, and Landon rolled his eyes. Gray, like hers.

"This is not a bad thing, Poky."

"So I guess I can't pull the 'I'm just a kid' thing, huh?"

"Nope."

"Too bad." Then he grinned again, and her heart went *kaplooey.* "So when can I come see your new house?"

"We already discussed this. Over fall break." Landon's new school was on some weird year-round schedule, so he got two full weeks off in October. "Did you get the pictures?"

"Yeah, it looks really cool." He frowned slightly. "Hey. You okay?"

Mallory's chest pinched again. Five years ago, Landon had been too young to fully understand the implications of the accident that changed all their lives. But more recently he'd apparently become more sensitive to her ongoing challenges, even though she rarely gave voice to them. Partly because the less she did, the less power they had over her, partly because she'd always detested complaining. Mostly, though, because she never wanted Landon to feel sorry for her. Or more importantly, that his mother's being in a wheelchair would have any negative impact on his life.

Sometimes, though, when the pain snuck up on her, she couldn't hide it from him as well as she'd like. And considering everything leading up to his new living situation, trying to pretend her life didn't affect his was probably naive. If not downright stupid.

"I'm doing okay, honey."

"Really?"

She smiled. "Yes, really. Okay, the move wore me out some, but it was worth it. It is so gorgeous out here. Sometimes you can drive for miles without seeing another car."

His brows crashed. "That must be weird."

Mallory laughed. "It is, a little. But you'd be surprised, how fast you get used to it—"

"Gotta go, Cristina's calling me to dinner. Talk tomorrow?"

"You bet, sugar."

The calls were never long enough. And every single time, when they ended, Mallory felt as if somebody'd hollowed out her chest. Which in turn made her question, yet again, whether she'd made the right choice, leaving behind her only child.

Except the only other option would have been selfish. If not downright cruel. Granted, the kid was a toughie, but she could tell he needed a break. Not from her, but from the attention she invariably attracted every time she set foot—or wheelchair—outside—

The landline's shrill ring made her jump. Mallory glared at the thing for a good second or so before wheeling over the tiled floor to answer it. A little testily, maybe. Why Mama'd insisted on installing the blasted thing, she'd never know, since they both had cell phones, for pity's sake.

"Hello?"

"Oh… I'm sorry," said a nice male voice on the other end. *Real* nice. Granted, in all likelihood it probably belonged to someone who did not match the voice, because that's the way these things usually worked, but a girl could dream. "I was trying to reach Dorelle Keyes?"

"She's not in right now," Mallory said in a somewhat less pissy tone. "May I take a message?"

A pause preceded, "Is this her daughter, by any chance?"

Mallory tensed. It was highly unlikely the paparazzi would've sniffed her out way up here, let alone unearthed an unlisted number. But these days she wasn't taking any chances.

"If you leave your name and number," she said, grimacing at her reflection in the mirror on the other side of the room, "I'll be sure to have Mrs. Keyes get back to you."

"It's Dr. Talbot. Edgar's vet? She'd asked me to check with my brother about a horse for her grandson?"

The relieved breath Mallory had been about to release snagged at the base of her throat. To hear Mama tell it, this Dr. Talbot would put Michelangelo's David to shame. And say what you will about her mother, the woman definitely knew *hot* when she saw it.

So much for not matching the voice.

"Um…you still there?"

Mallory wrenched her gaze away from her wretched reflection. Way too many nights of lousy sleep had definitely taken its toll. "Sorry. She was supposed to run that by me first."

"I take it you're Mallory, then?"

Call her crazy, but she was guessing this guy had no idea who she was. Meaning either he hadn't put two and two together, or Mama had—for once—kept her trap shut. Or maybe he was just playing it cool?

"That's me. Only nothing's been decided about the horse. Since we're still getting settled in—" a half-truth, since once the renovation had been completed all they'd had to do was dump stuff in closets and drawers and they were basically done "—I hadn't really given it much thought yet."

"Completely understandable. But if you are interested, my brother says he has a palomino that could be perfect for your son, especially if he's inexperienced. Not a youngster, but a lot of good years left. No health issues. Even-tempered as they come. And nobody knows horses like Josh—he wouldn't steer you wrong."

And neither would this man, she bet. Although how she'd deduce that from a five-minute conversation—and especially given her background—she had no idea. Something about his no-nonsense approach, maybe. But after so many years of never feeling as if she could truly trust anybody, of having to constantly watch her back—it felt... good. Even if it was only an illusion.

"I'm sure he wouldn't," she said, rearranging her long sweater over her thighs, even though her legs didn't really register the chill in the air. "But there are...logistics to take into account. I'm still not entirely convinced this is a good idea."

"Your mother said you grew up on a ranch, so I assume you know what goes into caring for a horse?"

His unwitting understatement made her smile. And ache, a little. An indulgence she rarely allowed herself. "I did. And I do. That's not the issue. But I honestly don't know how much time we're going to spend here." Her gaze drifted across the spacious family room opening to the flagstone patio and the pond beyond, its surface rippling gold from the reflection of the stand of yellow-leafed aspens on the other side of the property. Truthfully, the property had wrapped around her heart from the moment she'd opened the images in the Realtor's email. "And taking on a horse is a huge commitment."

"So this is a vacation home?"

"Something like that."

The vet was quiet for a moment, then said, "If it eases your mind, the Vista has excellent boarding facilities."

Mallory smiled, wondering what he'd wanted to say, but hadn't. "And you're an excellent salesperson."

He might've laughed. "Hard to make a decision without knowing all your options. Tell you what—why don't you and your mother meet me out there, see the horse for yourself? Make up your mind after that. You know where the ranch is, I gather?"

"I do, but…" Mallory paused. "I'll think about it. How's that?"

"Fine by me. But if you're serious I wouldn't wait too long. As great a horse as I suspect this one is? I imagine he's gonna find a new home without too much trouble."

"And would that be you trying to close the deal?"

"Just being up-front with you, Miss Keyes."

Nope, he had no clue who she was. Mallory smiled—she'd loved her work, heaven knew. And she'd appreciated being appreciated, no lie. But she'd found actual fame tedious at best and nerve-racking at worst. She'd never thought she'd live for the day when she wasn't recognized, but now that that day had arrived she felt positively buoyant.

But this business with the horse…a prod, Mallory thought this was. One initiated by her mother, perhaps, but clearly with the universe's approval: to get up off her duff—in a manner of speaking—and actually move forward with something instead of only talking about it. A bad habit she'd slipped into over the last little while.

But the move to Whispering Pines had been Mallory's idea, so there was that. Even though her decision had clearly flummoxed her poor Realtor. Why not Jackson

Hole? Or Vail? Or even Taos, if she had her heart set on New Mexico?

Mallory hadn't gone into details. Her reasons were her own. Not that she couldn't see the woman's point, that *here* was pretty much *nowhere*. Only, what no one understood, was that *nowhere* was exactly where Mallory needed to be right now. As in, somewhere where no one could find her. Watch her. Pity her.

Somewhere where she could truly start over. Some*thing* she'd avoided doing until now, even if she hadn't fully realized that. And some*times* starting over really did mean starting from scratch. From nothing—

And good Lord, she'd wandered off again, hadn't she?

"You know how much your brother's asking for… What's the horse's name, anyway?"

That got a low, rumbly chuckle. "Waffles."

"You're kidding? That's adorable."

"That's one way of looking at it. And Josh usually only asks for enough to cover his costs. We're not talking prize stud here or anything. The two of you can hash that out, if you decide to take him." Another chuckle. "The horse, I mean."

"Would tomorrow work?" Mallory pushed out of her mouth, surprised how hard her heart was beating. "I know it's Sunday, but—"

"No, tomorrow would be fine," Dr. Talbot said, sounding a little surprised himself. "I'll probably have my kids with me, though."

"Not a problem." Then she smiled, even as her heart twanged with missing Landon. "Boys? Girls?"

"Boys. Two of them. Loud. Constantly moving. Fight every five minutes. You've been warned."

At that, a laugh burst from Mallory's chest. "How about early afternoon, if that works for you?"

"One-thirty? That'll give us time to get home from church, get them fed."

Church. Sunday dinners. An ordinary life she dimly remembered. Missed more than she'd realized. "Sounds good." *Sounds wonderful...*

"Buzz at the gate, somebody'll let you in."

"Will do," she said, then ended the call, holding the phone to her chest as she heard the front door open. If she wasn't mistaken, that weird, tingly feeling in her chest was...excitement. Lord, she was in a worse way than she thought. Because damned if she wasn't looking forward to meeting this forthright-to-a-fault dude with the low, rumbly voice.

"Hey, honeybunch," her mother called out. "We're home!"

And no way on God's green earth was she sharing that tidbit with her mother.

Edgar's little nails scritched across the tile as he scurried over to Mallory, then stood on his hind legs so she could scoop him into her lap. Because she loved the scrawny little bugger beyond all reason. Mama followed shortly, fluffing her hair and wearing that look in her eyes that Mallory wished she could figure out how to banish once and for all. Not that she had anything against her mother's chronic optimism—heaven knows she wouldn't have made it this far without it—but all that cheerfulness did get tiring.

"So your Dr. Talbot called," she said, and Mama—who'd been unloading grocery bags onto the city-block-sized quartz counter in the kitchen—jerked up her head. Surprised, maybe, but not in the least bit guilty.

"My goodness, he works fast," she said, grabbing two jars of peanut butter and carting them over to the pantry. "I didn't expect to hear from him so soon." Shoving up her sweater sleeves, she returned to the counter, scooped up a half dozen boxes of pasta. "I assume he was calling about the horse?"

"He was. And thanks for cluing me in, by the way."

Mama gave her a look. "It wasn't anything I planned, for goodness' sake. But I was there, you know, with Edgar, and the thought popped into my head. Like these things do. I really didn't mean to go behind your back—" Her face fell as she clutched the boxes to her chest. "You didn't go and say something dumb, did you?"

Mallory stuck out her tongue, then sighed. "No, you'll be glad to know I managed to act like a civilized human being."

"Well, that's a load off my mind. So what'd he say?"

"That his brother has a rescue that might work."

"He does? How wonderful! Isn't Dr. Talbot the nicest man? And, oh, he has two of *sweetest* little boys. So what did *you* say?"

Mallory steered her chair into the kitchen and snagged an apple out of the bowl on the counter, polishing it against her jeans' leg before biting into it. Honestly, trying to follow her mother's train of thought was like playing pinball. Blindfolded.

"We have a date," she said, chewing, smiling slightly at her mother's gasp. "To see the *horse*, Mama. And you seriously need to give it a rest."

"Not a chance, missy. Not after what Russell did to you—"

"He didn't *do* anything to me. Which we've been over a million times. It just didn't work out. These things happen." Her mother made an if-that's-what-you-want-to-tell-yourself face. "It was for the best, Mama," she said gently. "You've got to let this go. I have." *Mostly.*

Tears welled in her mother's eyes. "You really think this is for the best for Lannie?"

"For God's sake don't let him hear you call him that.

And would you rather he live in a house where nobody was happy? Really?" Her appetite gone, Mallory wheeled over to dump the apple core in the under-counter garbage can. "Also, there's a new Mrs. Eames, as you may recall. So, onward and all that."

Mama's eyes brightened. "So does that mean—"

"No," Mallory said, knowing exactly what her mother meant.

"What am I ever going to do with you?" Mama said with a dramatic sigh, only to come over and plant a kiss on top of Mallory's head before collecting her dog and sashaying out of the room, leaving a trail of Giorgio in her wake.

Mallory smiled, only to release a sigh of her own. Because that was the question of the century, wasn't it? Not so much what Mama was going to do with her, as what she was going to do with herself. Since frankly she wasn't all that keen about spending the rest of her life without male companionship. Without love and affection and, okay, sex. True, things didn't work the same way they had, but they still worked. She definitely still…yearned, as Mama might say. But she wasn't so much of a fool as to think all she had to do was join an online dating service and—bam!— she'd be swarmed by seventy billion takers.

And not only because her legs were basically useless. There was also that whole who-she-used-to-be-before thing to take into account.

But to admit that she yearned—or dreamed, or wished, or whatever you wanted to call it—would a) make her sound as though she felt sorry for herself, which, *no*, and b) give her mother ammunition. Which, *hell* no.

Still. What was the harm in indulging a few tingles? A curiosity about the supposedly gorgeous man attached to the sexy-as-sin voice? A man with a sense of humor? And kids? Boys, no less? What was the worst that could happen? She'd get to spend an hour outside, on a beautiful fall day, with a decent guy. And she might even end up with a horse for her son out of the deal. Could be worse, right?

Heh. Maybe she didn't want to know the answer to that.

Chapter Two

A faint whiff of fireplace smoke tainted the cool, still air, mixing pleasantly with the smell of horse and dirt—the scents of his childhood, Zach thought. His life. What *home* smelled like.

"I can't believe you don't know who Mallory Keyes is," his brother Josh said as they stood in front of the fenced pasture where several of the horses grazed while they still could. In a few weeks the grass would be frozen, gone, and the horses would be on hay. Waffles was one of them, the early afternoon sun glinting off his pale gold coat. Yes, like syrup glistening over waffles. Behind them kids—and one ancient golden retriever—cavorted, as Josh's four-year-old boy, Austin, gave Zach's two a run for their money.

These days most of the fences were strung wire, of course. But this one, closest to the house, was still old-fashioned post-and-rail. A pain to keep in working order, but Granville Blake, whose family had owned this ranch in its various permutations for generations, wouldn't have it any other way. His nod to tradition, Zach supposed. Now, his forearms propped on the chewed-up top rail, Zach looked over at his smirking younger brother, Josh's choppy brown hair barely visible underneath his tan cowboy hat.

"So sue me. You know I don't keep up with that stuff."

"Except for a while there you couldn't go online for five minutes without seeing something about her."

"You couldn't, maybe."

"I'm serious. She was quite the hot ticket in Hollywood a few years ago. Well, more than a few years ago, I guess now." Josh paused. "You remember those Transmutant movies, when we were kids? When I was a kid, anyway, I guess you were a teenager by then. But I know you saw the first one, because the whole family went one Christmas. Anyway, she was The Girl. You know, the redhead with the big—"

"Josh." Zach's gaze darted behind them. "Kids."

"But you know who I'm talking about, right?"

"Maybe."

"Sure you do. Here…" He dug his smartphone out of his denim jacket's pocket, clicked a few buttons, then turned the screen toward Zach. His eyes twinkled. "Nobody forgets a…*face* like that."

Truth. *Now* Zach remembered, although he didn't think he'd ever known her name. Even when she hadn't been wearing her superchick costume, she was majestic, with all that red hair and legs that did not quit—

"Ring any bells?" Josh said, and Zach snorted. Chuckling, Josh slipped his phone back in his pocket. "Anyway, I think she went on to do more serious stuff afterwards. Maybe married a director or something? Even got nominated for an Oscar, I think. Not sure if she won, though. Mom would know. But she was hurt in a skiing accident a few years back. Right up there, in fact," Josh said, nodding toward the ski resort, tucked up into the mountains about twenty miles outside of town. "As in, career-ending hurt."

Zach frowned. "How do you know all this?"

Facing the boys, his brother shoved a hand in his denim jacket's pocket. "The question is, how come you don't? Seeing as we do share a mother. And anyway, it was big news here. Her accident, I mean—"

Liam took a tumble. Much wailing followed. Zach held out his arms as the three-year-old lurched toward him, bawling. "Now that you mention it," he said, hauling up the little guy, "it does sound familiar. But I guess I didn't pay attention to who it was. I was a little busy, getting the practice up and running, being a new father..."

Softly shushing his youngest's cries, Zach let the sentence fade away, unable to voice the rest of it: that he'd been so tangled up in love with his wife, his *life*, that the rest of the world basically didn't exist. Nor had he cared that it hadn't. Between those two little houses—his home and the clinic—he'd had everything he needed. And wanted. Getting caught up in pop culture was for people who had nothing better to do.

Except then Heidi was gone, and Zach was doing well simply to hold it together for his sons, his clients. By the time the boys were in bed he'd fall into his own in a dead sleep...until someone woke up, anyway. Extracurricular interests? Let alone activities? As if.

Josh's mouth twitched. "We really need to fix you up."

"You really don't. And you sound like Mom. Which is not a point in your favor."

"Whatever. There's this new waitress over at Chico's—"

"All yours, buddy."

His brother chuckled again. As well he should, considering he was every bit as much a target for the town's matchmakers as Zach. "So anyway. Yeah. This Mallory Keyes was a big deal at one time. Real shame, what happened to her. Funny that she'd decide to buy a place here. So close to where her accident happened, I mean. But people sometimes do weird things. How old you say her boy was?"

"Eleven."

"Then Waffles really should be perfect for him. Although I hope to heck they change the poor thing's name. Waffles? Honestly. Oh, that must be her... I guess Gus buzzed her in."

They turned in time to see the dusty-clouded approach of a high-end SUV, steel-blue with tinted windows. As Jeremy and Austin scampered off toward the house, Josh waved the car over; a few seconds later, it pulled up alongside the pasture and the window rolled down...and Zach nearly lost his breath. Especially when Mallory removed her sunglasses. And smiled. Now he remembered her, although his image was of a much younger version. A much less *finished* version. Mallory Keyes had what their mother would call good bones, all sharp angles softened by a full mouth, deep-set gray eyes and that hair. Holy hell, that *hair*—

Dorelle leaned over her daughter, grinning. "Hey, there, Doc. I take it this handsome young man is your brother?"

"Sure am," Josh said with a grin of his own as he walked over to open the driver's-side door. Dorelle apparently muttered something to her daughter that earned her an eyeroll and a "Really, Mama?" before Mallory extended her hand and they all finished with the introductions. Then, on a little gasp, she lowered her sunglasses. "Ohmigosh," she said to Zach, "is that your little boy?"

"One of 'em, yes. Liam."

"Well, hey there, sweetie," she said, her soft Texas twang curling right up inside Zach's chest. Then those dove-colored eyes lifted to his. "My mother said they were cute, but…wow. She did not—" her gaze shifted to his face "—exaggerate."

Now, Zach probably imagined it—because of that curling-inside-his-chest thing—but he could have sworn Mallory looked at him a trifle longer than necessary. Especially when her eyes seemed to jerk back to Josh. "Good to meet you both. Now if you'll give me a minute…"

Contorting her upper body to reach behind her, she retrieved a small, collapsible wheelchair from the back, deftly popping it open as she set it on the ground in front of her. "As you can see, I have mobility issues. So I hope I'll be able to get around in this?"

"Not a problem," Josh said without missing a beat. "The owner's wife was in a wheelchair for a while. The property's more accessible than you might think—"

By this time Mallory had maneuvered herself out of the car and into the chair. The car door shut behind her, she tented her hand over her eyes as Dorelle walked up to the fence, her floaty, lightweight sweater billowing behind her in the slight breeze.

"Is that him?" Dorelle asked, pointing. "The one who looks like a sunbeam?

"Sure is," Josh said.

"Ohmigosh, he's absolutely gorgeous. Isn't he, honey?"

But Zach was watching Mallory as she wheeled closer to the fence, her grace and determination colliding with what Zach realized was his own sudden awkwardness. As if he didn't know what he was supposed to think or do or say so he wouldn't put a foot in it.

Although why he should feel so unsettled, he had no idea. Wasn't as if he'd never seen anyone in a wheelchair before, for heaven's sake. But the image of the woman in front of him was such a stark contrast to the photo he'd just seen—

His phone to his ear, Josh signaled that he needed to

return to the house. "You go on and get acquainted, I'll be back in a bit—"

"Oh!" Dorelle signaled, then started after him, lickety-split. "You suppose I could use your restroom?"

"Sure thing, follow me…"

By this time Mallory was all the way up to the fence, leaning forward to clasp the middle slat. Waffles lifted his head, considering.

"Oh, my," she said on a breath, her hair glistening in the sun. "He's stunning, isn't he?"

Still holding Liam, Zach took a couple of steps closer. "He is that." As if he understood what was going on, Waffles moseyed closer to hang his head over the top rail, his ears twitching. "Come here, boy," Mallory crooned, angling herself close enough to raise her hand, chuckling when the horse lowered his head further to snuffle her open palm before lifting it again toward the baby. Zach tilted Liam closer and the horse tried to nibble the little guy's hair, making him giggle.

"He likes me," Liam said, giggling as he rubbed his slobbery head. Mallory laughed, the warm, gentle sound nudging open barely healed wounds.

"I would say so," she said, giggling herself when Waffles returned his attention to her. Fearlessly, she grabbed his bridle to tug him closer, touching her lips to the horse's velvety muzzle. "You're absolutely perfect, aren't you?" she said, laughing again when the horse "nodded" his agreement.

"You clearly have a way with horses," Zach said, hitching Liam higher on his hip.

"My daddy put me on my first one before I could walk," she said, the irony trembling in the air between them. "I was in my first junior rodeo at ten. But only because Daddy wouldn't let me compete until then."

"What in?"

"Barrel racing, mostly."

"Yeah?"

She grinned, which is when he caught the dimples. Or they caught him, he wasn't sure. "Now you know my secret. Used to have the strongest thighs in Texas," she said, patting the horse's neck again before wheeling away from the fence. "And, yes—" she looked up at Zach, her face squinched in the sun "—the irony is not lost on me. It's okay, I know what you're thinking."

Zach hesitated, then said, "What I'm thinking, is that I'm not sure if I should say 'I'm sorry' or not."

"You can say whatever you like, I've pretty much heard it all. And trust me, 'I'm sorry' is the least of it."

His nephew and his older son came into view again, along with Benny, their old golden retriever, who'd been recuperating on the veranda from the earlier hijinks. Liam wriggled to get down, then ran over to join them. The breeze got going again, rustling the drying leaves, tobacco-colored against the bright blue sky. Mallory looked up, a smile flitting across her lips before she shut her eyes. "Heaven," she said simply.

His own mouth pulling up at the corners, Zach squatted by her chair, ruffling the dog's neck when he trotted over, tongue lolling. "I think so. Although I suppose that makes me a rube."

"Hey." Opening her eyes, she smiled over at him. "In case you hadn't noticed, I don't exactly sound like royalty. Even after nearly twenty years in Hollywood. Not to mention God knows how many speech coaches, many of whom I'm sure I drove to drink." She looked out toward the other pasture again, her elbows resting on the arms of her chair. "One thing less I have to worry my pretty little head about, I suppose." One corner of her mouth edged up. "Not that I ever did."

"How'd you end up there?"

Benny nosed her hand, begging for attention. Mallory obliged. "You know, I honestly figured I'd live out my life right where I grew up. Probably marry a local boy, settle down on his ranch and pop out three or four babies who'd be born wearing cowboy boots. Except one day, there was this notice up at school about a production company needing extras for a movie being shot in the area. And some of us thought it'd be a hoot to go on over, see if we could make the cut. Earn a few bucks. Anything to break the tedium, you know?"

"Yeah, that happens around here a lot, too. Especially over the last few years. Movies shooting in the area, I mean."

"You ever do it?"

"Me? Oh, hell, no. I hardly ever see films, let alone have any desire to be in them."

"Which is why you had no idea who I was."

Despite the teasing in her voice, Zach felt his face warm. "Before my brother clued me in? No. Sorry."

"Are you kidding? It's a relief, frankly. And if I'd known then what I do now…" A sigh pushed from her lips. "But I didn't. And the bug bit. Hard. Even though being an extra is excruciatingly boring, suddenly the idea of becoming a ranch wife seemed even worse." She paused, not looking at him. "Or perhaps it was more that the ranch *boys* suddenly made my eyes glaze over."

"Ouch."

She shrugged. "I wasn't even eighteen, for pity's sake. And woefully sheltered. Even so, all it should have been was a few days' diversion. But due to a series of completely unforeseen events that started with that call for extras, I ended up with a one-in-a-million career." A funny smile tilted her lips as she watched the boys once more chasing each other around the field. "And a son I love more than life itself. What is it they say, about life being that thing that happens while you're busy making other plans?"

"Tell me about it," Zach said, and her eyes lifted to his, then scooted away again.

"Mama told me about your wife. I'm so sorry."

One side of Zach's mouth lifted. "Thanks. But you don't even know us."

"But I do know what it feels to have your life dumped on its butt," she said quietly, then snorted. "Literally, in my case." She nodded toward the boys. "How're they doing?"

Zach regarded her for a moment, wondering how she'd so effortlessly sucked him into a conversation he wasn't inclined to have with people he'd known all his life, let alone with someone he'd only just met. Wondering even harder why he'd let her. And yet...

"Liam—the little one—was too young when it happened to remember his mother. Jeremy was five, though. It was rough going there for a while."

"I can imagine." The dog laid his head on Mallory's knee, begging for attention. Smiling, she obliged. "After my accident, all I wanted was to make sure Landon knew everything was going to be okay. That we'd get back to normal again, even if it was a new normal." She paused. "Whether I ever did or not."

"Yeah. Exactly."

Grinning, she tilted her face to Zach. "Only a few weeks until he comes out to visit. I can hardly wait."

As obviously close to her son as she was, Zach was curious why he wasn't with her. The thought of not being with his boys made his blood run cold. But her reasons for leaving her son behind had nothing to do with him, did they?

Footsteps and chatter made him turn to see his brother and Dorelle returning. "I got a quick tour of the house," she said, smiling. "Met the owner, too. Between us we came to an agreement about the horse. He's yours, baby."

Mallory frowned. "What are you talking about? I thought we agreed—"

"We agreed it'd be nice to get Landon a horse. I don't recall any mention of who was supposed to buy him. And anyway, it's his birthday coming up. *You* can get him another video game this time."

"And I don't suppose you're gonna tell me what you paid."

"You got that right. And, yes, I made them promise to take the horse back if he doesn't live up to our expectations."

Josh rolled his eyes. "Like that wouldn't've been part of the deal, anyway."

Mallory looked to Zach. "You see what I have to put up with?" Except then she lifted her arms and her mother bent over to get her daughter's hug, even as Zach heard her whisper, "You're a pain in the butt, you know that? And what would I do without you?"

"Starve, most likely," Dorelle said, straightening up.

"It's true," Mallory said, looking from Josh to Zach, her eyes sparkling. "I hate to cook. Always have. Heck, I'd live on Cheese Whiz and crackers if I could. Love that stuff. Especially squirted right in my mouth. Because I'm all about efficiency."

Dorelle wagged her head. "Lord, *how* are you my daughter?"

A few minutes later, Mallory and Josh had worked out the details regarding the horse, who'd stay on the ranch until they had a chance to get Mallory's apparently neglected stable in order, and the women left. Watching the SUV disappear down the Vista's drive, Zach heard his brother chuckle behind him. He turned, feeling his forehead pinch.

"What?"

"Oh, nothing. Except you've got one helluva weird look on your face."

Zach opened his mouth, only to clamp it shut again. Because his brother was probably right. Not that he was about to give Josh the satisfaction. Especially since he wasn't sure he could explain what was going on inside his head.

So all he did was mutter, "You're nuts," before calling over his sons and dog and herding them toward, then inside, his truck.

But it was true, his head was buzzing. Even more than usual with the kids yammering behind him. And it kept buzzing for the rest of the afternoon and on into the night, even until after the boys were asleep and Zach was sitting out on his tiny back porch in the chilled night air, listening to the wind rustle the dying leaves and the dog snoring on the porch floor beside him.

The thing was, while Zach wasn't a people person like Josh or his mother—both of whom he swore fed off other humans like vampires sucked blood—he generally liked them well enough. Enough, at least, to deal with them on a daily basis in his practice. But he could count on the fingers of one hand the number of times he'd found somebody interesting enough to actually think about once he no longer had to interact with them. The one exception to that, of course, had been Heidi. Because, well, she'd been *Heidi*.

That he couldn't get Mallory Keyes out of his head now... What the hell? They'd barely even had what you could call a real conversation. Certainly nothing to provoke this crazy reaction.

This crazy *attraction*.

The thought made Zach actually jump. Oh, sure, she was pretty and all, but him noticing that wasn't unusual, even for him. He hadn't lost his ability to appreciate a good-looking woman, even if he no longer had any inclination to act on it.

And that was it, in a nutshell: because there'd never again be anyone like Heidi, someone who got him in a way nobody else ever had. The moment they'd met in school, even, the click had been almost audible. That kind of connection—what were the odds of that happening twice in one lifetime? Hell, even once? That his *once* had been ripped away from him like that…

His eyes stinging, Zach scrubbed a palm over his face. Sometimes he wondered if he'd ever stop missing her. Or at least if it would ever stop hurting so damn much. Not that he talked about it to anyone. What would be the point? Wasn't as if that would change anything, or bring her back, or make the hurting stop. And God knew he didn't need to dump his pain on anyone else. Especially his boys.

What Mallory'd said, about finding a new normal, especially for her son? Much to admire in that, actually. Just as there was a lot to admire in the woman. A *lot*. Come to think of it, maybe her strength was what he found so appealing. Well, that and her sense of humor. Had to admit, he was a sucker for a woman who could laugh at herself, who didn't take life too seriously—

Like Heidi.

Zach sighed so loudly he made the dog jump. Absolutely, he wanted nothing more than for his kids to have a normal life. To be *happy*, for God's sake, as kids are supposed to be. To have the kind of childhood he and his brothers had. As much as his boys could, anyway, with only one parent. But for him, *normal* died with his wife. That was just the way it was, nothing he could do to change it.

Just as he knew he'd never fall in love again. Because his *once* was over.

And not being able to get Mallory Keyes out of his head wasn't going to change that, either.

* * *

"Honey," Mama called from the other room, "have you seen my sunglasses?"

Wrapped up in a fluffy throw on a wicker couch—she refused to spend all her waking hours in the frickin' wheelchair—out in the glassed-in porch, Mallory called back, "Sorry, no."

"Shoot," Mama said, her ballet flats slapping against the brick pavers when she joined Mallory. "I know I had 'em when we drove out to the ranch, I must've left 'em in the powder room. And is there some reason you're sitting out here in the dark?"

Mallory felt a tight smile tug at her mouth. "Just thinkin'."

"About?" Enough light spilled through the great room's double door to see Edgar cradled against her mother's chest as she balanced a mug of something in her other hand.

She could, she supposed, refuse to answer. Or lie. Knowing her mother, both choices would be pointless. "How sad that poor man is."

Mama lowered herself into the padded rocker across from the couch. "I take it you're referring to our friendly neighborhood vet?"

Mallory smirked. "You know what's strange? Ever since this—" she gestured toward her lap "—I have a much harder time seeing other people unhappy. Almost like…"

"You can feel their pain?"

"Maybe."

"That's hardly surprising," Mama said, rearranging the spoiled rotten dog in her lap before reaching over to turn on a small lamp on the table next to her. Mallory winced. "Considering how hard you've worked to regain your own equilibrium, it's no wonder you're more empathetic. Now maybe you understand why I wanted the two of you to meet each other."

"Oh, I know why you wanted us to meet—"

"No, I don't think you do."

Mallory crossed her arms. "You're honestly gonna sit there and tell me you weren't trying to fix me up?"

"Not in the conventional sense, no. I'm serious," she said at Mallory's smirk. "Yes, I'd love for you to find a man who'll love you the way you deserve to be loved. I'm not gonna apologize for that. But even now that I know Zach Talbot is single, I'm not all that sure he's that man."

This was a shocker. "Really?"

"Really. Well, not now, anyway. Because when his brother and I were up at the house, he filled me in a little more about what Zach's been through."

"Oh, Lord, Mama—"

"I did not ask him, I swear. But Josh is clearly worried about him. So's the rest of his family, I gather. Zach's the oldest of the four boys—the second one's off finding himself or whatever, and then there's Josh and his twin brother Levi—"

"There's *two* of them?" With his dark good looks, Josh could put most of the Hollyhood hotties to shame. "Damn."

"You said it. But Josh and Levi are fraternal twins, Josh said. *Any*way…" She waved one hand. "Zach was always the quiet one, but since his wife's death, Josh says, it's like Zach's buried himself in his sorrow. Not that he ever was the life of the party or anything. More the serious type, you know? But for more than two years, it's like he's been in a fog. And the more Josh and I talked, the more it occurred to me you might be able to help him find his way out of that fog. As a *friend*, Mallory Ann. Only as a friend."

"And I'm supposed to believe that?"

"I do not understand why you always think I have ulterior motives."

"Um, because I've known you for nearly forty years?

But even accepting your premise…why do you think I'd be able to help him?"

"Because you've been where he is. Not losing a spouse, no, but having your world turned on its head. And you yourself said it hurts you to see others in pain—"

"That doesn't exactly make me an expert in helping them move past it. And anyway, I would think your situation is more similar to his than mine is."

Mama stroked the sleeping dog's head for a moment. "On the surface, that makes sense. But…"

"But what?"

Her mother's eyes met hers. "Your father and I…we weren't exactly what you'd call soul mates. Oh, we liked each other well enough, and we got along fine. Shoot, I can count on the fingers of one hand the times we argued. And I truly grieved him when he died. I mean that. Jimmy was a good man. But I remember the day—it was right after your tenth birthday, as I recall—when it suddenly dawned on me I wasn't in love with him. Never had been. I *loved* him, of course. Respected him, absolutely. And God knows I *wanted* more…" She shook her head. "It just never happened."

Frankly, Mallory wasn't nearly as shocked as she probably should've been. Mama was absolutely right about Daddy being a good man, and Mallory had loved him to pieces. And he, her. But her parents had had separate bedrooms for as long as she could remember. True, there'd been shared laughter, but it'd been more the laughter of friends, not lovers.

"And you're telling me this now, why?"

"Don't really know, to be truthful. Except something about being out here…it makes me want to be more honest, maybe. Must be the thinner air or something."

Mallory smiled. "So why'd you marry him?"

"Oh, you know. Small town, timing was right…" She

shrugged. "I had no complaints, though, all told. Don't think Jimmy did, either. Maybe because we didn't have any other frame of reference, I don't know. But my point is, if what Josh says is true—and my eyes and ears tell me it is—I can't relate to that young man's sense of loss, of upheaval, nearly as well as I think you can."

Wishing to hell the light was off, Mallory looked away. Because, fine, her mother was right—Mallory could definitely relate to the hurt she saw in those deep blue eyes, even though their situations were nothing alike. She also guessed Zach was doing everything in his power to keep everyone from knowing how much. Because she'd been there, too. Still was, frankly.

But what struck her even more was how close to home her mother's confession had hit. That even as Mallory found herself perturbed for her mother's sake that she'd apparently never experienced true, all-consuming love, she realized...neither had she. That her own marriage hadn't exactly been all about the passion, either. When it ended, she'd felt more disappointed than devastated. Had Russell felt even that much? she wondered.

And if she let her thoughts continue down this path, she'd be screwed. Hoping to ease the ache in her back, she fisted the cushion on either side of her hips to shift on the sofa. "And what, exactly, do you think I could do for Zach?"

"Be an example, maybe?"

"Of what? My spine is broken, not my heart—"

"Then maybe you should remember those first few weeks, after the accident, when you were sure your life was over. No, you're no expert, maybe, but you've overcome so much, baby—"

"Oh, Mama…"

"What?"

She reached for her mother's hand. "In case you hadn't noticed, my life has kind of imploded over the last year or so. Again. Whole reason I'm here, you know? To take stock, figure out what comes next. Maybe to you it looked like I was doing okay—"

"More than 'okay,' honey—"

"Physically? Yes, I've exceeded everyone's expectations. Not to mention my own. And I'm grateful for that, believe me. But my marriage fell apart, my son's living with his father, and I've been in career limbo since the accident. Those are the facts. I'm no more in the position to be a cheerleader for somebody else—particularly somebody I'm guessing would not take kindly to some stranger sticking her nose in his personal life—than the man in the moon. I came here to get away from complications, not pile more on."

"And it's not like you to feel sorry for yourself."

"Seriously?"

"Oh, don't give me that look—yes, that one. Because you know full well you wouldn't've made the progress you did if I'd babied you. If I'd felt sorry *for* you. And damned if I'm gonna start now. So you've had a few setbacks. Big deal. This, too, shall pass."

And the elephant swaggered into the room and plopped its big ole butt on the pavers between them.

"I know you think I shouldn't've left LA. Or given up on Landon—"

"I never said that."

"You didn't have to, the undertones to every one of our conversations are loud and clear."

Mama's mouth pulled tight. "Then, no, I don't think leaving was the answer. And it wasn't Landon you gave up on. It was yourself."

Mallory's face warmed. "Being realistic—or taking time to get my head on straight—is not feeling sorry for myself. Or giving up. Whether you think so or not. And what on earth does any of this have to do with Zach Talbot?"

Shifting the dog in her arms, her mother stood. "You need a purpose, honey. A reason to get up in the mornings. To get out of your own head. And right now it doesn't look to me like you have that. I'm only saying, that young man might be why you were led to come here."

"Now you're just talking crazy."

"Yeah, well, at least I'm talking. At least *I'm* facing the truth. Not running away from it."

With that, Mama shook back her hair as much as a ton of hairspray would allow and left the room.

But the worst part of it was that Mama was right. Dammit.

Then again, if Mallory was as messed up as her loving mother seemed to think she was, what on earth good would she be to Zach? Who by all accounts was equally as messed up?

She tossed aside the throw over her legs to get back in the chair, which she rolled across the floor to turn out the damn light, so she could sit in the damn dark and consider her sins.

Which, apparently, were many.

*Dam*mit.

Chapter Three

By rights, Zach should've let his brother return the sunglasses to Dorelle. Except Josh—rightly—pointed out that Mallory's mother would be far more likely to pay another visit to the clinic than Josh would get anywhere near where they lived on the other side of town. And since they didn't look like some cheapo discount store things, Josh guessed she'd probably like them back.

Sure enough, the next day Dorelle called, asked if Josh had brought them by. So naturally Zach said he'd be glad to return them to her since she had no reason to bring the dog in at the moment. No, of course it wasn't a problem.

So here he was, standing on the wooden-planked porch fronting the ranch-style house, set off far enough from the highway that the surrounding pinons and aspens easily swallowed up whatever traffic noise there might have been. It was real pretty out here, Zach had to admit, even though with two young boys and his practice he'd grown to appreciate the convenience of in-town living. Even if the town was Whispering Pines, where convenience was definitely in the eye of the beholder. Still—he turned, smiling at Benny watching the boys chase each other across a space far too large to be called a front yard—sometimes he missed living out in the country.

The front door—carved, huge, way overdone for the house—opened. In a dark green sweater that made her eyes go more hazel than gray, Mallory looked up at him, frowning. Zach lifted the sunglasses. She sighed.

"I swear, that woman loses more pairs of sunglasses. But you didn't have to bring them. We could've picked them up the next time we were in town—"

"She asked."

"Then I guess that explains the cookies."

"Cookies?"

"Three kinds, last time I checked." She leaned over to look past him. "And I take it the comets streaking across my yard are the boys?"

"They have two settings—warp speed and zonked out."

Mallory chuckled, but her smile didn't quite blossom full out. "Sounds familiar. Well, I suppose you may as well bring them in to eat the cookies. Because heaven knows I don't need them—the chair makes my butt look big enough, thank you."

Swallowing a grin, Zach turned and called. Panting and flush-faced, they ran over, the dog plodding slowly behind. Zach automatically started plucking bits of dried grass out of his youngest's hair. "You guys remember Miss Keyes from yesterday?"

"Uh-huh," they said in unison, doing the bobble-head thing as the dog finally finished the journey…and promptly planted his muddy front paws on Mallory's lap and started to lick her face, his tail pumping a mile a minute.

"Benny!" Zach bellowed over Mallory's shrieks and the

boys' explosion of giggles, grabbing the dog's collar and tugging. Hard. Like trying to move a five-hundred-pound boulder. *"Down!"* With a mighty yank, he finally got the dog off Mallory's lap. "And you two can stop right now," he said to the boys. Who of course only laughed harder.

Mortified, Zach turned back to Mallory, busy wiping dog slobber off her cheek. He dug in his jacket pocket for a tissue. Which, with drippy-nosed boys, he always carried. Amazingly, it was actually clean.

"I'm so sorry!" he said, handing over the tissue and glaring at the completely unrepentant dog. "I had no idea he'd do that—"

"No worries," she said, chuckling, mopping up the dog spit. "Come here, baby… No, it's okay, don't you pay any attention to the mean ol' man…"

The dog gleefully obeyed *her*, wagging back to again get in her face, grinning his doggy grin and clearly enjoying the hell out of her fawning all over him. A moment later Dorelle appeared, bringing with her the scents of chocolate and brown sugar.

"Oh, I'm so glad y'all came!" she said, snatching the glasses from Zach. "Can they have some cookies?" She beamed down at the boys. "Right out of the oven, all gooey and warm."

Two sets of pleading eyes swung to his, and Zach sighed. "Only a couple, they haven't had dinner yet."

"Got it," Dorelle said, gathering the boys to her like a mama hen and herding them toward the kitchen. "Y'all like milk with your cookies? Or juice…?"

Zach returned his gaze to Mallory, her lap still full of blissful dog. "Um… I wasn't actually planning on staying?"

"Meet my mother, the unstoppable force," she said, gently pushing the dog down so Zach could come inside, into a spacious entryway flanked by a living area on one side, a formal dining room on the other. Not that he knew much about decorating, but the overall effect seemed more yard sale hodgepodge than designer-contrived. Or maybe that was the contrivance. "Oh, and by the way, Mama's concept of a 'couple' probably does not jibe with yours."

"That's okay, neither does *my* mother's."

"And by 'not planning on staying,'" she said, her eyes sparkling as she looked up at him, "was that you just trying to be polite? Or do you really have someplace else to be?"

"Would it make any difference?"

"To my mother? Not a lot, no."

"And to you?"

Her eyebrows lifted. As did the corners of her mouth. "Far be it from me to detain a gentleman under false pretenses," she said with a slight bow. "Or keep him against his will. Although I'm sure you know my mother probably didn't leave those sunglasses behind on accident."

Zach shoved his hands in his back pockets, unsure about how he felt by this turn of events. Unsure, period. "I did have my suspicions."

Mallory glanced at the dog for a moment, then back up at Zach. "She'll swear up one side and down the other she's not trying to fix me up, but the woman lies like a rug."

He smiled. "So I take it you're not exactly on board with her plans?"

After a moment, she said, "The past five years haven't exactly been a picnic. All I want is a little peace, you know? Some space where nothing's happening. I am not looking for someone new in my life, believe me. At least not now." Her lips curved. "And I suspect," she said gently, "you know exactly where I'm coming from."

Her understanding rattled him more than he was about to let on. "I do. So the question is…do we tell your mother?"

"Oh, I suppose we should let her have her fun. She doesn't get much of that these days. And anyway, you seem reasonably sane, which is more than can be said for ninety percent of the men I usually come in contact with. The women, too, for that matter." Her eyes narrowed. "I feel like you and I could actually have a real conversation, if we put our minds to it."

Something like a tiny spark flickered in the center of his chest. "Then we don't have any pressing engagements."

"Good," she said, then started toward the large living room, the tile changing over to bare wooden floors. A doorway at the far end opened into what was probably a converted garage, through which he glimpsed a few pieces of exercise equipment. The dog plodded beside her, her new BFF.

"Nice place."

"Don't know about 'nice,' but it met the main criteria—right location, all on one level, easy access to the outside. It took surprisingly little to retrofit it for my needs. I know the furniture's goofy, but that's what happens when seventies' kitsch—my mother's stuff from our old ranch—meets I-don't-really-give-a-rat's-hiney. And, yes, the torture chamber vibe—" she nodded toward the exercise gear "—adds a nice touch, don't you think? Seriously, I have absolutely no style sense whatsoever. Nor do I care. And please, sit. Since I am. Of course, I always am, so there's that. Or we can go take a tour of the grounds, if you'd rather? I doubt Mama's gonna let your boys out of her clutches for a while."

Zach wondered if she always prattled like that. If he made her nervous. Although he could only imagine all the people she'd met over the years. Worked with. Why a country vet like him should discombobulate her, he couldn't imagine. But if getting outside put her mind at ease...

"Sure. Josh asked if I'd check out the stable conditions for Waffles, anyway. He's pretty protective of the horses that leave his care." He grinned as she led him through a glassed-in sunroom and onto an obviously new deck that looked over a small pond. "And every bit as bad as your mother."

She belted out a laugh that made him smile. "You saying we're doomed?"

"That'd be my take on it, yep."

"Family," she muttered as Benny collapsed in a patch of sunshine on the deck and promptly passed out. "Can't live without 'em, can't kill 'em. Aw…poor guy. He's not exactly a pup, is he?"

"Nope. In fact, he's closing in on fourteen."

"Get out!" she said, chuckling when the dog released a deep, contented breath. "He's in fantastic shape for an old dude. You've obviously taken great care of him."

"Actually I've only had him a few months, since his owner passed away. She made me promise to take Benito if anything happened to her. Since she was in her nineties, it was touch-and-go which of them would leave first. And she was worried about what would happen if he ended up in a shelter." Squatting beside the golden, Zach gently stroked the warm fur. "Not many people want to adopt older dogs."

His eyes still closed, Benny lethargically thumped his tail, then lifted his head to give Zach's hand a quick slurp before drifting back to sleep. Zach stood, smiling for the old dude. "So how could I not make whatever time he has left as good as possible? And he and the kids are inseparable."

"I can see that. Then again, dogs and boys are a match made in heaven."

He looked over to see a gentle smile creasing Mallory's face as she watched the dog. "You've got a pretty soft spot for them, too, I'm guessing."

"I was raised on a ranch, remember? We always had dogs. Four or five, at least."

"But Edgar's your mom's?"

"He is. We had three pups, back in LA. Rescues, all of 'em."

"Breeds?"

"Mixed. One big, two medium. They're with my ex. Or more to the point, with Landon. Because no way was I going to separate them. Poor kid's been through enough, he can keep the dogs. Well. On to the stables?"

"Sure."

Her shoulders bunched under the sweater as she navigated the gently sloping ramp leading to what looked like a recently poured cement path, the autumn sun turning her hair nearly the same color as the early-frost-kissed sycamore leaves overhead. "I actually closed on the place three months ago. Took some time, though, to get this all done. And my Realtor was a jewel, supervising it all."

"It looks like it was always like this."

"That was the idea. You ever been here before? For the previous owners, maybe?"

Zach shook his head. "Property's been vacant for years. Twenty, at least." He stopped short of the stables—four stalls, what looked like a good-sized loft—to take in the spacious dog runs, a sturdy chicken coop. And beyond them, a small orchard. Tart cherry trees, probably. Several types of apple. Whatever might actually produce fruit at this altitude.

Then he glanced over at the stables, and she said, "Yes, I've already checked them out. They're fine. Although I probably won't bring the horse over until closer to when Landon gets here. Since Waffles needs to be ridden. And it's not like I can simply hop up on the saddle and take off."

For the first time, he heard in her voice, if not exactly fear, at least apprehension. A stark contrast to the persona she otherwise presented. To him, anyway. But not only was it none of his concern whether she got back up on a horse or not, he hardly knew the woman. Still, he was surprised how mad it made him, that she'd let fear get in the way of doing whatever she needed, wanted, to do.

Like he had room to talk.

He let his gaze roam over the property, which seemed to go on for a while. "How much land you got here?"

"About twenty acres. After LA, I wanted some space. *Needed* it."

"You miss Texas."

"More than I wanted to admit, yeah."

"So why didn't you buy a place there?"

"Didn't miss it *that* much," she said, and he smiled.

"What are you going to do with all of this, though?"

"Haven't decided. Doubt I'll entertain much, so I don't feel any pressure to spiff it up. Although the landscaping could stand some tending. You know anybody who could do that?"

"I'll get you some names."

"Good. Thanks." She paused, her hands folded in her lap. "But I'm sure you're not the only one who wonders why I chose to buy up here."

"Because of what happened, you mean?"

She smiled. "Let me guess…your brother?"

"When we were discussing the horse, yeah. As for other people wondering about it…" He shrugged. "None of their business. And if anybody gets up in yours…ignore 'em."

Looking back, Mallory thought it was almost scary how naive she'd been when she'd first arrived in LA. How easily she'd trusted people she'd later discovered did not deserve that trust. Twenty years on, she was far more cautious. Far less likely to take anyone at face value.

But something about this man resurrected all that old…

innocence, she supposed it was. She knew in her bones she was safe with him, that he was as honest and pure as the landscape that had wrapped itself around her soul from the moment she'd seen it.

"I bought a house here," she said, "because I fell in love with the area fifteen years ago. The accident didn't change that."

"Was that before or after the first Transmutant movie?"

A laugh burst from her chest. "After. By several years. But oh, Lord, what I wouldn't give to expunge those from my history." She cocked her head. "So you've seen them?"

He smiled. "Only one, when I was a teenager. Although I'd apparently expunged it from mine," he said, and she laughed again, then sighed.

"I was *so* young. Barely legal. But both Russell—"

"Russell?"

"Eames. My ex. The director?" Zach shrugged, and she smiled. "Anyway…he and my agent swore it was a good deal. And by the third release, it was a *very* good deal, money-wise." A hawk fluttering overhead made her look up. "Although by rights I should've been pigeonholed as The Hot Chick and my career would've been over before I was twenty-five. Russell's taking a chance on me beyond that, that I could do something different… I was extraordinarily fortunate."

"No wonder you married him. If he had that much faith in you."

A smile pushing at her mouth, Mallory looked out over the wooded ravine dropping off twenty feet from the path. "He really did." Because that much, at least, was true. "And yes, I suppose that was a major reason why I did marry him. Even though everyone thought I was nuts, what with his being only a couple years younger than my father and all. But for a long time, Russ was everything to me. My champion, my protector, not to mention my acting coach…" She released a breath. "For that much, I'll always owe him a great deal."

"So what happened?"

She shrugged. And hedged. "Ultimately we couldn't adjust to our new roles. As simple as that." Her mouth twisted. "Russell's new wife is even younger. Gorgeous. Ridiculously smart. Not in the industry. And Landon likes her. You know, now that I think of it, I think I hate her."

"Can't imagine why," Zach said, and she snorted. Then her eyes met his. "It was a damn good run, you know? I had a career most people can only dream about, and God knows I never expected." Half smiling, she squinted back at the forest. "And no matter what happens from here on out, nobody can take that away from me."

After some moments, she heard Zach sigh. "I know what you mean. All the good stuff…it really is ours forever, isn't it?"

"It really is," she said softly.

"Do you miss it?"

Mallory met his gaze again. "Sometimes. All the insanity that goes with it?" She shrugged. "Not so much. And I don't only mean what actually goes into making a film. That has its moments, sure. Magical ones, actually, when suddenly a scene comes together…" She smiled. "There's a reason I kept doing it. Well, other than the fact that I had absolutely no skill for anything else. Aside from barrel racing, that is. But the *world* of movie-making… it can be hard. And weirdly far less real at times than the make-believe one up on the screen. Even so, I'll admit to wishing the decision to quit had been mine."

He leaned one hand against an apple tree trunk, glancing up into the tangled branches before facing her again.

"And now?"

Was it strange, that she understood exactly what he was asking? "It's funny—at first I worried that after everything I'd worked for, I'd fade into oblivion. That it'd be as though I'd never existed. Then I found myself *hoping* people would lose interest, move on to the next thing. And yes, you do start to feel like a *thing*. A commodity. When that didn't happen, I realized all I wanted was to be left alone to deal with my life in peace. But mostly for Landon to be left alone to live his."

"That why you left him with his dad?"

There was no censure in his voice. At least none that she could hear. And certainly she saw nothing but compassion in those gentle blue eyes, so calm and steady behind his glasses. Then a short, dry laugh escaped his lips.

"Sorry, what was that I said about people getting up in your business—?"

"It's okay. And actually it feels good to talk about it."

"You sound surprised."

"It's not something I usually do. Only child and all that."

"No friends?"

"Other than my mother? Not really, no."

Still leaning on the tree trunk, Zach shoved his other hand in his pocket, his gaze tangling up with hers so hard she lost her breath. "So tell me about Landon. If you want to, I mean."

At least, that's what Mallory thought he'd said. Hard to tell through the buzzing between her ears. Jeebus. In a few short sentences, this stranger had offered more of himself, been more accepting of *her*, than Russell had over their entire relationship. She'd had no idea they even made men like that.

And hellz, yeah, you better believe she was going to take advantage of it.

"Leaving him behind was the hardest thing I've ever done," she said over the lump in her throat. "But all the attention was really beginning to take its toll on the kid.

Especially as he got older. The paparazzi never left us alone. Never. It was ridiculous—I have no idea what they thought they would see, what I'd do that would've been even remotely interesting, let alone fascinating. But wherever we went, there they were. No matter how much I tried to evade them."

"That sucks."

"You're telling me. Even if Landon didn't say anything, I could tell how hard it was on him." A huge sigh pushed from her lungs. "What I said before, about only wanting him to feel normal? That's all I'd ever wanted for him, even before all this. So his dad and I decided it would be best for him if I removed myself for a while."

"Did you consider taking him with you instead?" he asked gently.

"Of course. But the kid's life is there. Friends, activities…" She smiled. "His dad. Who can't leave the scene. Or doesn't think he can. And directors aren't sexy from a gossip perspective. Seriously, how often do you see Steven Spielberg or Ron Howard's picture on the front page of *The National Enquirer*? I was much more intriguing, in a let's-all-pity-the-gimp kind of way. And I'm allowed to say that, being the gimp and all."

"And your boy's happier?"

"I think—hope—he's at least more…at peace. And honestly? I'm still questioning whether I made the right choice. But it was the only one I felt I could. I'd do anything for that kid. Anything. I'm sure you know what that's like."

His lips barely curved. "All too well."

Mallory smiled back, then released another sigh. "At least Landon knows it's not permanent, that it's kind of like when I'd go on location and he'd stay behind, or only come visit from time to time. As much as he remembers that. If all goes well, the sharks will move on to other feeding grounds and I'll be able to return undetected. In the meantime we talk at least once a day, if not more. I haven't abandoned my child. Even if it sometimes feels like I have."

At that, she saw something new in his expression. Almost…annoyance, if she had to name it. Not that she was surprised. No matter how many knots she twisted herself into trying to explain, she doubted few people would understand. Then he reached up and twisted a Gala apple off a nearby tree, holding it out. "Want one? I can't guarantee it won't be mealy, this time of year, but—"

So she'd gotten the wrong end of the stick, maybe? "No, thanks, got a whole bowlful inside. And the ones we've eaten so far have been perfect. Tart and sweet at the same time."

"Like memories," Zach said quietly, frowning at the apple for a moment before taking a bite.

"I suppose so, yes."

Not looking at her, he chewed for a moment, then nodded, wiping a trickle of juice on his sleeve. "You're right." He waved the apple at her. "Perfect."

"Then please take some home with you, there's no way we'll ever eat them all."

"I might do that. Thanks." He took another bite, then said, "I should probably go."

"Ah."

Zach frowned. "What?"

"We talk about why I left my son behind and two minutes later you suddenly need to leave?"

"No," he said slowly, "it occurred to me we've left *my* rambunctious boys with your mother, who's probably more than ready to be rescued by now."

"Really?"

The frown deepened. "You don't seriously think I'm judging you?"

"I think it'd be weird if you weren't."

"Call me weird, then. Mallory…nobody can truly know what they'd do in someone else's shoes, but it's obvious you didn't make that decision lightly. Or that you were only thinking of yourself. You're only doing the best you can. Same as every other parent in the world. And something else—whether Landon fully understands it or not right now, you've set an example of how the best choice isn't always the easiest. In fact, it rarely is."

It was several moments before she could speak. "Wow."

He shrugged. "Something I remember my parents drumming into us. Just thought I'd share."

Mallory smiled. "My daddy used to say the same thing, actually. So…thanks. But please don't feel you have to leave on my mother's account. When she's had her fill of little boys—" she wagged her phone "—she'll let me know. Trust me, that woman is in hog heaven right now. And your boys probably are, too. That woman has grandmothering down to a fine art."

Chuckling, Zach slid down against the tree's trunk to sit in a patch of mottled sunlight—sending a shudder of silly pleasure through her. She had nothing to offer this man—other than apples and cookies, maybe—and yet he was still here. How long had it been since someone other than her son had wanted to be with her for her own sake? Warmed her right down to her unfeeling toes, it did.

Zach smiled—and oh, my, did he have a nice smile— when Benny appeared, wagging his tail. "Hey, guy…" He ruffled the dog's head. "Good nap?" Benny sniffed the apple, actually shook his head, then lay down in the dirt at Zach's feet as he nodded toward the dog runs.

"I seem to remember the previous owners raised purebred Labs. I think Granville may have even gotten one for his daughter. Hey—maybe you should think of fostering, yourself. You certainly have the space for it."

Mallory stared at the runs, imagining. "Wouldn't that mean a full-time commitment?"

"Not necessarily. And God knows the local shelter would be grateful for anything you could do. It's no-kill, so they get overcrowded from time to time."

"Let me…think about it."

"Fair enough." Zach took another bite of apple, rubbing the dog's rump with the toe of his boot as he chewed, then threw the core into the ravine as her phone pinged— a text from Mama.

"She's asking if we'd like to join them."

One side of Zach's mouth lifted. "Her way of saying she's reached her limit?"

"Not that she'd ever admit that."

Chuckling, Zach pushed himself to his feet, brushing off his butt as he walked toward her. "Yeah, it's all fun and games until somebody slugs somebody. My own mother regularly threatened to put us up for sale. Unfortunately for her, we knew it was a hollow threat."

They started back toward the house, Zach's stride comfortably matching her wheelchair's pace. And right then, in this perfect setting with this incredibly sweet man walking beside her, Mallory felt almost…whole.

A moment to cherish, for sure.

Zach had just buckled the boys into their car seats when Dorelle came scurrying out to the truck, an enormous plastic container clutched to her chest.

"Cookies," she said, a little breathlessly, practically shoving the container into his hands.

"For the entire town?"

"I might've gotten a little carried away."

Zach smiled. "Well, thank you. My mother used to bake up a storm until my father had a heart attack—"

"Oh, no—"

"It's okay, it was some time ago now, and he's doing great. But things like cookies are pretty much off-limits. And no sense in tempting the poor man, she says. Anyway, there's a whole bunch of us who have no problem with cookies, so these won't go to waste, believe me."

She beamed. "I'm so glad. Enjoy—"

"Can I ask you something?"

The question had popped out completely without his brain's permission. Except if it hadn't, it would've bugged him like an invisible thorn that hurts like hell even though you can't see it.

Dorelle forehead puckered. But only slightly. "Yes?"

"Any reason why Mallory hasn't ridden recently? Plenty of paraplegics ride," he said when her mother's brows lifted. "Seems to me, as much as she obviously loved it—"

"Don't you need to get the boys home?"

Zach propped a hand on the truck's roof, glancing inside to check on the kids, both of whom had conked out. So much for getting them to bed on time tonight. "I've got a minute," he said, returning his gaze to the brunette, who sighed.

"To be honest, she hadn't ridden in years, anyway. Not since she left Texas. Oh, wait, that's not entirely true— she did have to ride some for one of her movies. But for pleasure? No. And of course, since her accident..." She shook her head.

Something like frustration knotted in his chest. "Somehow Mallory doesn't strike me as the type to let much get in the way of whatever she wants to do."

After a moment, Dorelle pushed out a tiny laugh. "That child was the most headstrong little girl you ever saw, I swear. A trait that only got worse the older she got. Used to drive her daddy and me nuts. If not to drink, on occasion. But that's what made *her* driven, too. Made her such a fierce competitor, because she demanded so much of herself." A sad smile curved her lips. "Of *life*. So when she took up with Russell Eames, took off for Hollywood at eighteen, not only did we know there was nothing we could say to dissuade her, but deep down we knew she'd be fine. Because like you said, she wasn't one to let anything, or anybody, get in her way. And as headstrong as she was, at least she wasn't foolhardy."

She stuffed her hands in the pockets of her long sweater. "And after the accident—once the initial shock wore off, at least—she was the most determined human being you'd ever hope to see. At first, anyway. Let me tell you, she surprised the pants off of everyone in the rehab facility. But anymore…"

"You think she's given up?"

"I think maybe on top of everything else the divorce hit her harder than she wants to admit."

"She said the marriage hadn't been working for a while."

"Not sure it ever really did, to be honest. Still. Aside from being the director on that first picture she did, when she was an extra, not to mention being the one who took her under his wing and got her career off the ground, Russell was her first love. Her only love, for all that. Or close enough to it to count. But whatever's clogging up the works, I've definitely seen a change in her. One I doubt she even sees in herself." She smirked. "Except you know how unlikely it is for a child to listen to their parent. Especially a long-since-grown child. Besides which she'll only insist she's fine, that I'm overreacting."

The worry in her eyes touched something deep inside him. A worry he'd seen before, in his own mother's eyes. About all four of her sons, for one reason or another. And not for nothing, had she worried. "You're very trusting," he said, "sharing all this with a stranger."

"Except you don't feel like a stranger, Dr. Talbot. Don't

know why, but you never have." She paused. "But thank you for letting me share. I really don't have anyone to do that with anymore. Oh, there's one sister in Idaho, but we haven't really talked in years. And of course I've been focused on taking care of Mallory recently. Not that I'm complaining," she hurriedly added. "And I know I could've gone out and made friends in LA if I'd wanted. I just didn't."

He smiled. "Then we'll have to make sure you find friends here. My mother, for one. Annie, the owner of Annie's Place in town. But as far as your daughter goes..." He glanced toward the mountains, then back at Dorelle. "If it's any consolation, I get the feeling that headstrong little girl is still in there somewhere."

"Well, honey, if you could somehow help me find her," Dorelle said, smiling, "I'd be more than grateful. And you know what? I think she'd be grateful, too. But you did not hear that from me. Enjoy the cookies," she said, then headed back toward the house, her arms tightly wrapped around her waist against the evening chill and leaving Zach wondering what the hell he'd gotten himself into.

He got into the truck, his heart turning over in his chest at the sight of his sleeping sons behind him. Hell, he could barely find himself these days, let alone anyone else.

Yeah, well, maybe you should try harder, whispered a voice inside his head.

Clenching his jaw, Zach rammed the truck into Reverse and backed out of Mallory's drive, that voice hanging on tighter than a prizewinning rider on a really pissed-off bull.

Chapter Four

A week later, that conversation about why she'd bought property up here still bounced around underneath Mallory's skull, all nice and tangled up with images of the man she'd had the conversation with.

So much for finding *peace*.

True, Whispering Pines seemed as good a place as any for a vacation home, for all the reasons she'd given Zach. But she couldn't deny that most of what had driven her away from LA had followed her here like a bunch of imprinted ducklings. Except not nearly as cute.

Not that she didn't truly love it here, she thought as she drove into the circular drive fronting the Vista's main house, then cut the engine to her modified SUV. The landscape was everything she remembered, and more— bold and vast and in your face, the colors so intense they burned. And she couldn't wait to show Landon around, get his take on the quaint little stuck-in-time town, the sky that went on forever. His room up at the house, which she and Mama had taken great pains to fill with as much New Mexican kitsch as they could fit in a twelve-by-twelve room, right down to the lassoing cowboy wallpaper. She smiled—he'd probably think they'd lost their minds. And he'd be right.

The lightweight wheelchair reassembled and ready to go, Mallory lowered herself into it and shut the car door, then rolled up the gently sloping drive toward the main house. Not that she'd planned on it, but when she'd called Josh earlier about seeing the horse again, he'd mentioned that Granville Blake, the ranch's owner, had wondered if he might meet her. It would have been ungracious, to say the least, to say no. She'd even "made an effort," as Mama would say, dragging out her nicer jeans and boots for the occasion, a fave vintage fringed suede jacket, a pair of dangly handmade silver earrings she'd picked up from a local artisan some years back.

A lovely piece of Southwest history squatting in the shadows of the Sangre de Cristo Mountains, the house was equally breathtakingly magnificent and unpretentious, the earthy stucco dabbled in flickering patches of sunlight filtered through a half dozen huge, yellowing cottonwoods. Sturdily supported by a dozen rough-hewn posts, the clay-tiled overhang sheltered a flagstone porch spanning the entire front of the hacienda. And scattered across it, a mishmash of manly rocking chairs and traditional *equipales*—those drumlike curiosities peculiar to northern New Mexico, tanned pigskin seats and backs over wood-latticed bottoms—beckoning a person to sit and enjoy the view. She caught a whiff of woodsmoke—piñon, most likely, the sweet-smoky scent a welcome change from LA smog.

The front door opened right as she hiked the chair's front wheels to access the porch, which thankfully was nearly level with the paved drive.

"You mus' be Miss Keyes," said a beaming older man, his stomach straining against a plaid flannel shirt and nearly obscuring a silver belt buckle the size of a fist.

"That's me."

"I'm Gus, the housekeeper," he said, standing aside so she could steer through the heavily carved, oversize front door. "Mr. Blake and Josh are in the office, I'll let them know you're here. Can I get you anything?"

"No, I'm good. Oh, my," she said, taking in the enormous living room, anchored by a floor-to-ceiling stone fireplace on one end, while the wall opposite the entryway was basically all glass—a trio of French doors opening onto what appeared to be a courtyard. The furnishings were what she'd call Expensive Macho Casual—lots of leather, wrought iron, Native rugs and artifacts, all precisely placed over Saltillo pavers she guessed had been there forever. "This is beautiful."

"Thank you," said a slightly breathless male voice behind her. She turned the chair to face Josh and his employer... also seated in a wheelchair, as it happened. But from illness, she quickly deduced from the sallow skin, the sunken cheeks. The oxygen tubing. Still, underneath a thatch of short, salt-and-pepper hair, the older man's bright blue eyes sparkled. The motorized chair whirred closer—she got the feeling he wasn't used to it yet—and he leaned to take her hand in his, his grip stronger than she would have expected, but cool. "Granville Blake."

"Mallory Keyes."

"Oh, yes, I know. I've seen most of your movies," Granville said on a slight wheeze. "You're one talented young lady. Not to mention even prettier in person than on screen."

Mallory smiled, inwardly blessing him for not speaking of her career in the past tense. "You're very sweet for saying so. Thank you." She glanced up at the beamed ceiling punctuated with a pair of iron chandeliers worthy of a hotel lobby. "I'm guessing there's a history here?"

"There is indeed. My great-granddaddy built the original main house in the 1880s, before New Mexico was even a state. This here's an add-on, from the twenties. Since then not much has changed, from what I can tell from photos. Only what wore out." He smiled. "Although we did update the bathrooms from time to time. The ladies are kind of particular about those."

"We are that," she said, and Granville chuckled.

"So I hear you've bought Waffles."

"Technically, my mother did. But yes. For my son, when he comes to visit."

"It was Josh's idea, fostering horses." His smile softening, he glanced up at the young man, his eyes shining with pride. "A damn good one, too," he said, then returned his gaze to Mallory as she caught the young man's almost diffident shrug. "He tells me you're letting the horse stay here, though."

"For the time being. Probably until Landon arrives. But I couldn't wait to see him again."

Granville's eyes narrowed. "Josh tells me you used to ride."

"Yes. I was raised on a ranch, in fact."

"You don't say? Cattle, horses…?"

"Both. Not a huge operation, but it kept us out of trouble."

"A real cowgirl, then?"

She laughed. "At one time."

"From cowgirl to movie star." He shook his head. "Life certainly takes some strange twists and turns, doesn't it?" His chuckle ended on a brief coughing spell. "Well. I'll let you and Josh to it. There any of that vegetable soup left, Gus? I think I might like that for lunch…"

She watched as Josh's boss and the housekeeper left

the room, then turned to Josh, frowning. Sighing, Zach's brother screwed on his cowboy hat and led her back outside, walking slowly enough for her to easily keep up.

"We don't know, exactly, what the problem seems to be," he said when they reached the end of the porch, answering her unspoken question. "Mainly because he won't discuss it. Or let anyone who comes in to help him discuss it with us."

"Why on earth not?"

"Because that's the way he is. Always has been. But it's pretty obvious things're going downhill fast. Just in the last few weeks."

"I'm so sorry. He seems like a wonderful man."

"He is. Dad was the ranch manager when we were kids, so we all grew up here. Granville was more like an uncle than a boss. And when Dad had his heart attack and couldn't work anymore, Gran deeded him the house my parents now live in."

"Does he have family? Do they know?"

His hands slugged into the pockets of his jeans jacket, Josh stepped off the porch onto a cemented path leading to the pastures and barns, his head angled so she couldn't quite see his face in the hat brim's shadow. "One daughter. She lives in DC. I can't even remember the last time she was home."

"But doesn't she know…?"

"I have no idea," he said, not looking at her. Not meanly, exactly, but definitely as though she'd crossed a line she didn't know was there. Even so, he tossed her a tight, almost apologetic smile. "I'm only the hired help, not my place to get involved in family business." *Only the hired help, my butt*, Mallory thought as Josh nodded toward the nearest pasture, where Waffles was out with several other horses. "Well. May as well go see your boy…"

She'd forgotten how much intrigue and craziness there

could be in a small town. Like a living soap opera. Even as a kid in Springerville, Mallory had been aware of far more than a child probably should've been. But what else was there to do, other than watch TV and go into town every now and then? Of course, this wasn't Springerville and it was highly unlikely that, as an outsider, she'd ever really be privy to the town gossip. Oh, she knew *that* drill. One did not air one's dirty laundry to strangers, ever. However, that didn't mean she was immune to the emotional pull—that a man's courage in the face of his obvious illness wouldn't tug at her heart; that a younger one's equally obvious sting over a young woman's absence wouldn't pique her curiosity.

That his brother's obvious pain over the loss of his wife wouldn't make her thoughts drift in directions they had no business drifting.

As they neared the fence several of the horses, including Waffles, plodded over to the fence to say hey. Her chair's wheels bumped a bit on the uneven surface as she pushed herself close enough to talk to the handsome boy. And his scent, his feel when she laid her cheek against his muzzle, stirred up all manner of emotions she wasn't sure what to do with.

Not all of them related to the horse.

Grinning, Josh leaned one elbow on the fence's top rail. The other horses, realizing this wasn't about them, walked off, nickering and whuffing among themselves. "Easy to tell you're a horse person. You've got that look."

An echo of his brother's words, her first time here. Mallory smiled when Waffles nodded, as if he was agreeing with Josh. "And what look would that be?" she said, reaching into her jacket pocket for a piece of carrot, which she offered to the horse, palm up.

"That one. You came prepared."

"I'm no fool," she said, and he chuckled. A nice laugh,

the kind that probably made girls go all moony on a regular basis. He had that way about him, the good-looking
cowboy who thought he was all that. The off-kilter grin,
the cheek creases when he smiled…so not her type, she
thought, slipping the horse another piece of carrot. Even
if she hadn't had at least a good ten years on him. Which
of course got her to thinking about his older brother, who
by rights shouldn't have been her type, either—

"So where's your little man?" she asked, remembering his son.

That got the beaming smile of a man only too happy
to talk about the most important person in his life. "Right
now? Austin's with my folks. But it varies, depending on
who snags him first. He's a pretty popular little dude. So
when's *your* boy coming out?"

"Two weeks," she said, flashing a smile at Zach's
brother.

"Let's see…two weeks. Before or after the tenth?"

"After."

"Too bad. He'll just miss the rodeo."

"There's a rodeo?"

"After a fashion. Probably nothing like you were used
to." At her lifted brows, he said, "Zach told me. Barrel
racer, huh?"

"Yep." She patted the horse's shoulder and steered the
conversation away from herself. "What about you? You
ride?"

"Some. Cutting, mostly, these days. Although since
Austin came I've only done the local one. It's a big deal
around here, though. Which is why I cannot figure out
for the life of me why my brother and his fiancée decided
that's when they should get married."

Mallory's head jerked up. "Your brother?"

A grin spread across Josh's mouth. "My twin. Levi.
What?"

Her face hot, Mallory turned back to the horse. "For a moment I forgot you had more than one brother, that's all. But a wedding!" she said, smiling at him again. "How exciting!"

"For Levi, maybe," Josh said with another quick grin, propping a boot up on the lower rail and looking out over the pasture. "Levi'd been sweet on Val all through high school, but she ended up with his best friend. Then both Levi and Tomas enlisted, went to Afghanistan..." He sobered. "Except Tommy didn't make it home."

"Oh, no..."

"Yeah. Everybody here took it pretty hard. He was a good guy. A really good guy. The kind of good guy who makes his best friend swear to look out for his wife and kids."

"Oh. Wow. And now they're getting married."

"Yep."

Waffles nuzzled her hair. Looking for more carrots, maybe. Mallory obliged. "You all really watch out for each other, don't you? The whole town, I mean."

"To the point where we drive each other nuts sometimes. But yeah."

Mallory hesitated, then asked, "Would it be betraying a confidence to tell me what happened to Zach's wife?"

Frowning out into the pasture, Josh waited a good long time before answering. "Car crash. Hardly a secret. Beyond that, though..."

"Understood. And there's no reason he should talk to me about it, really. We hardly know each other. But I get the feeling he doesn't talk about it to anyone."

Josh turned his gaze to hers. "No. He doesn't."

"That's too bad."

"I think it's a family trait. Except for my mother. Whatever she's feeling, you know it, boy. Which doesn't mean she blabs about anyone else. But the rest of us..." His head shook. "None of us even know what really went on with Levi, when he was overseas. Although I suspect he's sharing more with Val than he ever did with any of us. She has that effect on people."

"Aw…you like your sister-in-law."

Another cute, almost embarrassed grin preceded a quiet, "We all do. She's good folks."

Mallory smiled. From what she'd heard so far, there were several people in town she thought she might like getting to know.

"A word of warning, though," Josh said. Kindly, she thought. Leaning one hip against the fence, he crossed his arms high on his chest. "Zach's doing a pretty good job of holding it together. For his kids, his clients. At least, that's how it seems to us. But the minute you poke at him, you're right—he'll close up faster'n a snapping turtle. And despite what most women think—and with good reason, I'll admit," Josh said with a smile, "not *all* men are totally oblivious. Meaning I can see you're curious. Don't know about interested," he said, his eyes narrowing, "but the wheels are definitely turning."

She blew a short laugh through her nose. "Yes, they are. And you're right, I am curious. In a people-fascinate-me kind of way."

"And the other?"

Her gaze shifted to his. "Speaking of looking out for each other."

Josh shrugged. "Long ingrained habit. Whether any of us want to be looked out for or not."

And sometimes, she decided, lying really was the best option. Because to admit the truth would only go to prove it wasn't only her legs that weren't working properly. "Your brother is obviously a nice guy, and it hurts me to see someone else hurting," she said, echoing what she'd said to her mother. "But I won't pry, I promise."

"And that's really all there is to it?"

"Yes." *No*. But the more details she went into—that she was only there part-time and would return to Los Angeles, that she was in no position to embark on a relationship herself—the more likely she'd sound as though she was protesting too much. Never mind that both things were true. And of course there was the indisputable fact that her wheelchair was a huge turnoff for some men. Okay, a lot of men. For her, it was freeing. There were few places she couldn't go, far fewer things she couldn't do than people might realize, even if she did them differently. But an awful lot of people only saw her as somebody who couldn't walk, as though that was the main thing that defined her.

Still, there was the also indisputable fact that the man stirred something inside her that went way beyond her severe hanky-panky deprivation. Something that took her out of herself, made her...want to do more. Be more. But to say this was a nonstarter didn't even begin to cover it.

And the look Zach's brother was giving her right now told her he wasn't buying it for a minute. Especially when he said, "That's too bad. Because I think you'd be real good for him."

"Ex*cuse* me?"

Josh laughed, then nodded toward the nearest barn, a modern number, all mental and clean lines. Nothing like the much, much older—and far more charming—huge wooden structure she'd noticed on her way up to the main house. "If you need tack for the horse, his previous owners gave us what they used for him, and you're welcome to it. But you might want to see it first, decide if you'd rather get something new for your boy..."

At least this stuff she knew, Mallory thought a few minutes later as she inspected the hardly worn saddle, the bit and bridle and blankets that were part of Waffles's "dowry." This stuff, she could make decisions about.

The rest of it? The important stuff? Thirty-eight years, she'd been doing this, and she still knew bupkiss.

Especially about why in the hell she'd find herself interested in the last man on earth who'd be interested back.

Some days, Zach mused as he ushered his very wiggly progeny into a booth at Annie's, being a responsible adult was beyond him. As in, the kind of adult who actually cares about what his kids are shoving in their faces. Only after the morning he'd had—which had started at o-dark-thirty hauling ass out to Ed Jenkins's place to help his mare deliver a breech foal—he was doing well to feed the kids at all. Heck, remember he had kids.

"Hey, there, Zach. Boys." Val Lopez, Levi's fiancée, appeared at their booth, order pad at the ready and a smile on her face that put the sun to shame. In the early afternoon light streaming through the street-facing window, her long, wavy ponytail was the color of corn silk. "What'll it be? Wait, let me guess," she said, setting a pair of kids' paper place mats in front of the boys, a small round diamond flashing on her left hand. "Regular burger and fries for this one," she said, tapping a giggling Jeremy on the head, "chicken fingers for cutie-pie there, and a deluxe cheeseburger with double fries for you. Am I right?"

"Are we really that predictable? Liam—no, buddy." The baby was on his knees, the ketchup bottle already upside down over the place mat.

Grinning, Val shoved the pad in her apron to calmly reach over and pry the plastic squirt bottle from Liam's chubby hands. "Most men are, honey," she said over the baby's affronted bellow. She reached into her pocket for a small packet of crayons, plopped them in front of the boy. "Y'all want chocolate shakes with that?"

"Please." Zach smiled tiredly as Jeremy leaned close to his baby brother, helping him to choose a crayon to color the horse in the center of the place mat. Blue, apparently.

As Liam began to madly scribble more or less over the horse, Val called out their order to AJ, Annie's husband and the diner's short-order cook, before turning back to Zach. They were on the late side for lunch, so the place was virtually empty except for a couple of tourists a few booths down and Charley Maestas, the old army vet who spent a good portion of every day at the counter, mostly shooting the bull with whoever would talk to him. Which was pretty much everybody. Yeah, the town definitely looked out for their own.

"So how'd Ed's mare do?" Val asked. "She okay?"

As tired as he was, Zach had to smile. "Now how'd you know about that?"

"Your mom was in for a second, filling up her thermos on her way out to the pueblo to deliver a baby. Said you'd dropped the boys off before dawn."

"I did. And mare and filly are both fine."

"Excellent. And you?"

"Nothing a four-hour nap wouldn't fix."

Even as she laughed, sympathy swam in Val's eyes. A single parent herself, she knew what it was like, trying to juggle child care with working. Especially in a small town with limited day care options. "Hey. I'm off at three. If you want I'd be happy to take the boys. They can play with the girls for a couple of hours. In fact, y'all could even stay for dinner. Levi's probably gonna give the grill one final whirl before it gets too cold. Whaddya say, guys? You wanna come over and play with Josie and Risa later?"

Jeremy looked up, all bright eyes and snaggle-toothed grin. "Cool—"

"Thanks," Zach said, "but I'm good."

Clearly, exhaustion was making him cranky. Not to

mention stupid. But honestly, as much as he loved his brother—and his soon-to-be sister-in-law—he didn't think he could handle four children under the age of eight right now.

No, let's be honest—what he couldn't handle was watching how happy his brother and Val were. And if that didn't make him a rotten brother, not to mention a terrible person, he didn't know what did. For crying out loud, they were both great people who'd been through hell. God knew if anyone deserved a happy ending, it was those two. As well as Val's two little girls.

Except even he knew his funk had nothing to do with them, even if his brother's engagement had made Zach that much more aware of his own loneliness, of how desperately he still missed his wife. Especially at times like this, when he simply felt like there wasn't enough of him to go around, when his kids needed more than he had to give—

He felt Val's hand on his shoulder. "Hey. No playing the martyr allowed."

"I'm not—"

"Trust me, been there, got the T-shirt. So you're coming over and that's that. You wanna go pass out upstairs, that's okay. We'll handle the kids. All you have to do is hang on for a few more hours."

He released a weary laugh. "Fine," he said, and Jeremy gave a fist pump. He and Val's oldest were about the same age and loved nothing more, apparently, than verbally sparring with each other. About *nothing*—

"Hey, there," Val said brightly as the bell over the door tinkled. "Sit anywhere you like—"

"Oh, my goodness! Dr. Talbot?"

In a blur of fluttering fabric and jewelry, Dorelle made a beeline for him while Mallory hung back a few feet, her lip caught between her teeth. Embarrassed? Amused? Hard to tell. But the twinkle in the redhead's eyes, those damn dimples, made Zach's chest thump. In a not entirely unpleasant way, actually. The wind had messed up her hair, which she was trying to smooth back down. Then she tugged a strand of it out of her mouth.

And suddenly Zach wasn't nearly as pooped as he'd thought he was.

"Imagine finding you all here!" Mallory's mother said, giving Jeremy a quick side hug. Which, amazingly, the kid didn't seem to mind. "And I thought we were pushing it, getting here so late for lunch! What a beautiful blue horse, Liam!"

By this time Mallory had pushed herself close enough to mutter, "Laying it on a little thick, Mama?" which earned her an eyeroll and a gentle swat. In spite of himself, Zach chuckled. And despite spending so much time in barns, he hadn't been born in one. So he wriggled out of the booth, then gestured toward it.

"Join us? No, no, it's okay, we don't even have our food yet. And there's plenty of room." He looked at Mallory. "Really."

Dorelle looked extraordinarily pleased. But it was Mallory's lifted eyebrow that made his chest thump a second time.

A lot harder than he would've expected.

Chapter Five

Mallory had been relieved to discover the little town was actually pretty wheelchair-friendly. Yes, there were laws about that, but unfortunately some business owners weren't above skirting those laws as much, or as long, as they could. At least until they got caught. But she'd been able to roll into every place they'd gone that day without too much problem, and the diner was no exception. Even sitting at the end of the booth wasn't particularly awkward.

Sitting three feet away from Zach, however, was another issue entirely.

Not that he wasn't as polite as always. Friendly, even. And he was the one who'd invited her and her mother to sit with them, although she wouldn't go so far as to say it was his idea. Again, polite. His mama had raised him well. But all the good manners in the world weren't enough to erase the tension in the set of the man's jaw, the sadness lurking behind his tired smile. How damn hard he was *trying*.

Just kill her now.

Such a gentle face, she thought, stealing a glance at his profile as he quietly, but firmly, put the kibosh on Liam's attempts to stuff French fries up his nose. Gentle, but strong, too, shouldering his obvious pain with grace and courage.

Tears stung Mallory's eyes as she tried to choke down a bite of her own burger. Sometimes, this empathy stuff was for the birds—

"You okay?" Zach said, his low voice startling her. She glanced over to see her mother deep in conversation with the boys before pushing out a little breath. Nodding. Wanting to laugh, actually, that his concern for her stemmed from hers for him.

Welcome to irony.

"I'm fine," she said, figuring if she could convincingly pull off playing a homeless transgender prostitute surely she could pull off one little white lie. Okay, so maybe not so little. "I remember that phase with Landon," she said for Zach's ears only, nodding toward the little boy, now completely enchanted by her mother's drawing horns on the blue horse. "The orifice-plugging phase, I mean. You name it—if it fit, he shoved it up there. Beans. Rocks. Chocolate chips. Although at least those melted. But oh, dear Lord, what a holy mess *that* was."

Zach laughed, and she smiled. Then her mother announced that, since she and boys were finished, she was taking them outside to run off some steam in that adorable little square across from the restaurant.

"You two take your time finishing up," Mama said. "Nobody's in any hurry…"

After they left, Mallory bit off half a French fry, then sighed. "I'm so sorry."

"That your mother took my kids? I'm not."

"You're very trusting."

"That she'll bring them back? Absolutely."

Mallory chuckled, then gobbled up another fry. Holy cow, these were good. "Actually, what I meant was—"

"I know what you meant. And no worries—"

"Y'all doing okay over here?" Val said, swooping by to refill Mallory's water glass.

"You kidding?" Mallory said, brandishing a fry. "I can't remember the last time I had fries this good. And this burger *rocks*."

The cute little blonde grinned. "AJ'll appreciate that, I'm sure—"

"And you have to have a piece of Val's pie," called out an equally thin, but older woman on the other side of the counter.

Val blushed. "Annie, really?"

"We've still got…let's see…" Adjusting her chained glasses on her nose, Annie peered into the glass dessert case. "Apple and peach, looks like. And chocolate crème. Pickings are pretty slim this time of day." She let her glasses drop. "But still good."

"The chocolate, then," Mallory said.

"Excellent choice."

"Honestly, Annie," Val said on a sigh, then gave Mallory an *I'm so sorry* look. "Please don't feel obligated—"

"To eat a piece of chocolate crème pie? Not a problem."

"And apple for you, Zach, I presume?" Annie called, already removing two pieces from the case. "Plain or à la mode?"

"Plain. Please."

A second later Val set their respective choices on the table by their plates, then cleared the boys' and Mama's places before swooping away again. Mallory gawked at the three-inch-high confection, and Zach chuckled.

"Somebody looks like she's seriously contemplating not finishing her lunch and going straight for dessert."

"The thought had occurred to me," she said, and he

smiled again. And if she wasn't mistaken, at least some of the tension seemed to have sloughed off his shoulders, faded from his eyes. "There's a real 'everybody's family' thing going on here, isn't there?" she said, prying off a piece of her burger and popping it into her mouth.

Zach got quiet for a moment, then said, "We'd be idiots not to be at least *friendly* to strangers, since a good chunk of our economy depends on tourist dollars."

"Good call," Mallory said, trying to ignore the slight twinge of disappointment that the banter hadn't been personal. Then again, how could it have been, considering she hadn't been in the town but five minutes? After all, Whispering Pines was only a temporary escape for her. But for all these people, it was home.

Zach took a bite of his burger, then set it on his plate, wiping his hands on a napkin, looking as if he was weighing whether he should say what he was thinking. Her burger finally finished—or close enough—Mallory shoved away the greasy plate and reached for her prize. "What?" she said, and he slightly jerked.

"I just keep thinking how tough it must've been, after your accident. Especially right after. Not only on you, but your son."

Wondering what had prompted this twist in the conversation, Mallory took a bite of her pie…only to almost choke on her gasp of delight. A small smile curved Zach's mouth.

"Amazing, right?"

"As in, oh. My. God."

He nodded toward Val, cleaning up after the couple who'd just left. "She makes 'em. From scratch. Crusts and everything."

"Wow." Making a mental note to get that girl's number, Mallory took another bite, swooned all over again, then decided to address Zach's comment.

"Landon was only six. And before, I'd always wrestle and roughhouse with him—I was a bit of a tomboy, anyway, so I was beyond thrilled that God gave me a son—" Reaching for his own pie, Zach smiled. "But then I couldn't. Not at first, anyway. And I think for a long while he wondered where Mom had gone. Suddenly he had no idea how he was supposed to act with me. What he could and couldn't do. What *I* could and couldn't do. And of course I wasn't sure, either, at first. So there was a lot of feeling our way with each other for a while."

"But I assume you did."

Her eyes filled again; annoyed, Mallory grabbed her napkin and dabbed underneath her lower lashes.

"I'm sorry," Zach said, "I didn't mean to bring up a sore subject—"

"It's not that. It's..." She blew out a sigh. "No matter how prepared we think we are for life's curveballs, we never really are, are we?"

Zach blew out a long, weighty sigh. "Nope. Not by a long shot."

"And it's about more than simply coping with the changes. It's about... Oh, Lord, this is going to sound silly..."

"I doubt it," Zach said, smiling.

She snorted. "You haven't heard it yet. But I was going to say, it's about learning from them. Becoming stronger."

Not looking at her, he took a large bite of his pie. "Whatever kills us and all that?"

"Exactly. I think we're all a lot tougher than we believe we are. But unless we're tested, we'll never find out, will we?" She paused, then said softly, "And if you don't mind my asking...what brought this on?"

He leaned back against the seat, his arms crossed as he chewed. "Not entirely sure," he said, swallowing. "Although maybe..." One side of his mouth tilted before he met her gaze. "Maybe I feel I could learn something from you?"

And she'd thought she'd been thrown for a loop before. "Me?"

"Not that I'm equating our situations, I don't mean that. Only that we've both had, as you say, curveballs thrown at us. And you..." There went that gentle, soul-shattering smile again, God help her. "You seem to have found what I'm still looking for."

It took a minute to find her voice. "And what would that be?"

His eyes locked with hers. "Acceptance."

To hell with this, she thought, reaching for his hand. Never mind they barely knew each other, or that they were in public, or...or a million other reasons why she shouldn't. The man needed to be touched, dammit. And she was handy.

"Okay. For one thing, I've had longer to adjust than you have, so there's that. For another, maybe it's...well, *easier*'s not the right word, but...this is just my body, you know? It's not...*me*. Granted, there were all sorts of ramifications that happened as a result of the accident, and for a while I was pretty depressed, not gonna lie. And don't kid yourself, it's not all one big party going on inside my head. I have my moments. Days." Her mouth screwed to one side. "Months. Even so, from where I'm sitting— heh—losing the ability to walk is nothing compared with losing a piece of your heart. And I don't have to know details to know that's what happened."

Zach's eyes watered, and she thought, *Oh, crap*. He blinked, though, and cleared his throat, before letting go of her hand to pick up his fork again, only to hold it suspended over the pie. "Maybe so. But I am so tired of feeling like this. Like I'm half living. When I realized I was in love with Heidi..." A smile ghosted around his mouth.

"That we were in love with each *other,* I'd never been happier. And every minute we were together…it was pretty damned amazing."

Mallory smiled. "Please don't tell me you never fought. Or got on each other's nerves."

Laughing softly, he finally took another bite of his pie. "Sure we did. Sometimes. But never over anything important, you know? In any case," he breathed out, "it's like you said—we're never really prepared for those shifts in the universe. Our universe, anyway. And when she died, I had no idea how much losing her would hurt. Could hurt." His gaze met hers. "Would still hurt, even after all this time. And all I know is, I will never, ever let myself go there again."

"Oh, Zach—"

Except whatever she was about to say caught in her throat as something like surprise bloomed in his eyes.

"You know, I've never said that before. To anyone."

"Not even to your family?"

"*Especially* not to them. They wouldn't…they wouldn't get it. But you have no idea what a huge relief it is to say it to *somebody.* So thank you."

For what? she wanted to say as the bell jangled and the boys burst back inside, out of breath and giggling, Mallory's mother laughing almost as hard as they were. But after the initial stab of annoyance at the interruption, Mallory had to admit she was actually glad the conversation ended when it did. Because what would, *could* she have said? After all, she'd be the first to admit she'd never loved that deeply. And to be honest, seeing how tortured Zach still was this long after his wife's death she wasn't sure she ever wanted to. Nor could she blame him for wanting to steer clear of emotional involvement again.

Even so, there was a big difference between accepting your circumstances and rolling over and playing dead.

Giving up. God knew Mama had drummed that into her head enough those first few weeks. Months. But if her own experience was anything to go by, that was one of those things you had to learn for yourself, on your own terms and in your own time. In other words nothing she could say would make a lick of difference if Zach wasn't ready to hear it.

Never mind how badly she wanted to swat him upside the head. Or that she wasn't deeply touched that he'd opened up to her, even if she didn't completely understand why. Even so, she thought as she excused herself to use the ladies' room, she could only hope that something or someone would eventually free him from what was obviously a crushing pain.

"Oh, sorry!" she said when she pushed open the door, smacking it into Val's hip.

"No worries," the waitress said, grinning. "Major design flaw. The stall's good for you, though. Annie had it enlarged and retrofitted some time ago."

"Thanks."

She wheeled herself inside, began the tedious process involved in simply going potty.

"So…looked like you were having quite the conversation with Zach. Sorry—I forget not everyone is cool with talking while they're peeing—"

As opposed to asking about a private conversation. Got it. "That's okay, I'm good. This takes a while, anyway. I thank God every day it's not a timed event."

She heard a low chuckle on the other side. "And I just now realized," Val said, "how nosy I sounded. I only meant, it was nice to see him talking to *somebody*. Somebody not related to him or a client, I mean."

Mallory smiled. "It's a small town. Kinda limits the options."

"True. Even so…" She heard water running. "He needs to get out of himself more. We all worry about him."

The stab of irritation took Mallory by surprise, especially considering the obviously genuine affection that had provoked the comment. Finally done, she pulled herself back together and made her cumbersome way to the sink to wash her own hands.

"You're going to be Zach's sister-in-law soon, right?"

Val looked a little puzzled, even as she smiled. "In a couple weeks, actually. Who told you?"

Mallory swiveled around to reach the paper towels. "Josh. When I was out at the ranch the other day." Wiping her hands, she tilted her head and said gently, "I gather you went through some pretty rough times yourself."

"You might say," she breathed out.

"Then you get where Zach is coming from."

"But that's my point—I do know. And I also know I wouldn't've gotten through it without the support system I had. Which is what we're all trying to be for Zach."

"I can see that. And like you, I don't even want to think about how I would've managed without my mother. I'm more grateful than I can say that she was there for me. But she couldn't work through whatever I needed to work through *for* me."

Val leaned on the sink, her cheeks puffing out with the force of her breath as she looked at Mallory in the mirror. "I guess when you've been through it yourself it's even harder to watch someone else suffer like Zach is. But I hear what you're saying. And you're right. Absolutely. Hey…" She turned to face Mallory, her eyes sparkling. "Would you and your mama like to come to a cookout at my place later?"

"I don't…what?"

"Nothing fancy, just Levi and me and our girls, and Zach and his boys. Maybe the guys' parents, not sure about that yet. Depends on whether or not one of Billie's clients goes into labor. You like kabobs?"

"Um, sure. But…"

"Look, if you two are gonna be spending any significant time here…well. It can get a little *too* quiet, you know?"

"Never mind the quiet is exactly what I came for. Not that I don't appreciate the invitation, but…"

"Got it. But if you change your mind…here…" Val tugged her guest checkbook from her apron pocket, scribbling something on the top slip before tearing half of it off and handing it to Mallory. "Here's the address. It's not far from here. And don't worry about if there's enough food, Levi always cooks enough for half the town, anyway. And to be honest? As much as I love my family, and this town, a little fresh blood now and then doesn't hurt. But it's up to you."

Mallory took the slip, more touched—and more conflicted—than she could say. She stared at the number for a moment, then smiled up at Val. "Let me have your number, I'll let you know for sure a little later. How's that?"

The blonde lit up like a Christmas display. "That'll work, sure."

They exchanged numbers on their cells before finally leaving the restroom, Val heading into the kitchen, Mallory toward the booth where her mother sat. Alone.

"Zach and the boys left?"

"The little one was clearly done," Mama said, getting to her feet. "I told him to go on, not to wait on my account. Although I was beginning to wonder if you'd disappeared into an alternate universe. You okay, baby?"

"Yes, I'm fine. Got caught up in a conversation with Val, that's all."

"In the ladies' room?"

"Seemed as good a place as any."

Shaking her head, Mama rearranged various pieces of clothing, then lugged her elephant-sized purse out of the booth and headed toward the door. "Zach picked up the check, by the way. I told him that wasn't necessary, but he insisted. Wasn't that nice?"

"Yes, it was," Mallory said, letting her mother get the door for her. They were all tucked up in her mother's car, however—Mama had insisted on driving the Caddy today, and Mallory hadn't had the wherewithal to argue—before Mallory said, "Val invited us to dinner, by the way."

Clutching the steering wheel, Mama turned, her brows drawn. "When? Tonight?"

"Uh-huh."

The thing was, until she heard the words fall out of her mouth she hadn't decided whether or not to tell her mother about the invitation. After all, she could have kept the whole thing to herself and no one would've been the wiser. But even though her mother hadn't said anything, Mallory knew the isolation was beginning to get to her. Especially after already not having many friends in LA. Unlike Mallory, who could happily go for weeks without interacting with the human race, Dorelle Keyes was born to schmooze. For all she'd sworn Mallory was doing her a favor, taking her in—and on, let's be real—after the accident, Mama had made the far greater sacrifice. Especially by trekking out to the middle of nowhere with her daughter. Add that to everything else the woman had done for her? Sucking it up and going to someone's backyard barbecue was the least she could do.

"Why?" Mama asked.

"I have no idea."

Her mother looked out the windshield, the beginnings of a smile curving her red lips. "Who all's gonna be there?"

"Most of the family, sounds like. You game?"

Mama looked at her again, then reached over to curve her warm fingers around Mallory's hand. "Are you?"

"Sure. Why not?"

"Then, hell, yes," Mama said, backing out of the lot hard enough to make Mallory's stomach jerk six ways to Sunday. Although that probably had less to do with her mother's sketchy driving than the fact that Zach was part of that *most of the family* thing.

And she really, really needed to get over herself.

Growing up in this family, Zach mused as he sat on his parents' back patio watching four kids run around the yard in the rapidly waning light, a person got used to plans changing at a moment's notice and for the slimmest of reasons. In this case, moving dinner here instead of having it at Val's house. Something about his parents having a bigger grill, she'd said when she called.

Whatever. Had nothing to do with him. He was only here for the boys, so they could play with their new cousins, hang out with their grandparents. Well, that, and because he was hardly going to turn down another opportunity to feed said boys without actually having to cook for them. These days, his main goals were to keep them alive and out of trouble. However those were accomplished, he thought as he stretched out on a webbed lawn chaise he remembered from when he was a teenager, he wasn't too picky about.

He let his eyes drift closed. He never had gotten that nap, and while he wasn't about to actually go pass out in his parents' guest room, at least he could rest easy knowing there were as many alert adults as kids. Except the minute he did, the muffled sounds of the kids' giggles and the adults' conversation over by the smoking grill lulled him into that not-entirely-comfortable state of half-consciousness where reality smudged into memories, where Val's laughter sounded eerily like Heidi's. Where, for a split second, he thought she was standing over him, chuckling about his having fallen asleep.

Zach jerked awake, his heart pounding, to see his mother sitting across from him, a gentle smile on her high-cheekboned face. The sun had all but set by now, gilding her long, silver hair, her favorite bulky cardigan, buttoned nearly to her neck against the evening chill.

"When did you get here?" he said, fighting a yawn as he sat up straighter.

"A few minutes ago. Had a gal thought she'd started labor, but I don't think so. She's not five minutes away, though, I can get to her quickly if things change. There's beer in the fridge. Wine, too, although you probably don't want that. I restocked when I heard we were suddenly hosting a party."

Zach frowned. "Since when is family a 'party'?"

"Since Valerie decided to invite that actress and her mother." At Zach's apparently flummoxed expression, Mom's smile spread a little farther. "You didn't know?"

"Nope."

"Is this a problem?"

"Why would it be?"

"I have no idea. But I can never tell with you these days."

"And what exactly is that supposed to mean?"

"Maybe you should listen to yourself," Mom said, pushing herself out of the chair, "and get back to me on that. Anyway, I expect they'll be here soon." A frigid breeze shunted through, ruffling her hair. Hugging herself, she looked out over the yard. "Think we should eat inside? It'll be awfully tight, though."

"It'll be fine, Mom," Zach said, prying himself out of his chair. Steeling himself for... God knew what. Okay, not true, because he knew damn well what—for the first woman since Heidi who, simply by virtue of being herself, could apparently make him lower barriers he'd sworn were never coming down again. Who could turn a simple conversation over burgers and fries into…more. A lot more. Who looked at him like she could see into his soul.

Whose eyes let him see into hers.

Over the cramp to his chest, he smiled at his sons stomping across the patio toward him, a panting Jeremy clutching his chest as if he was about to keel over, even as he held on tight to his little brother's hand.

"What's with you?" Zach said, hauling Liam into his arms, his chest cramping all over again when the little boy yawned and snuggled close, his sweet-sour smell tickling Zach's nose.

"Worn…out…" Jeremy said, the chaise squawking when he collapsed on it. "Josie and me were chasing the baby. Hers, not ours. How can something with legs that short run that fast?"

"Exactly what your mother and I used to say about you when you were that age. You were like a little lizard, darting away from us so fast we could barely catch you. Especially if you got hold of something you weren't supposed to have."

Breathing a little easier now, Jeremy looked up at him. "I sorta remember."

"I doubt it. You wouldn't even have been two."

"No, really." The boy sat up, his expression far too serious for a kid. "It's fuzzy, but… I think I can hear Mom's laugh."

Somehow, Zach held it together. From inside, he heard his brother give his father good-natured grief about something, his mother tell them both to behave. Then, faintly, the doorbell ringing. "Not from then, I don't think. You were five when…she was with us until you were five."

Looking out into the now dark yard, Jeremy nodded. "You still miss her?"

"Every day."

"Yeah. Me, too," he said, then got up. "It's cold. We should go inside. Where it's warm."

Where, crowded in his parents' tiny kitchen with everyone else, were Mallory and her mother, Val making introductions as both women effortlessly worked the crowd. Still holding Liam, Zach hung back, watching, unable to take his eyes off Mallory, who'd taken baby Risa onto her lap and was now making faces at her, her eyes alight. Even in a plain black sweater and blue jeans, with not a whole lot of makeup that he could tell, the woman…glowed. As if she was more than a mere mortal. And not only because the overhead light made her hair look like it was on fire. Whatever it was that held his attention captive, it came from someplace deep inside her, he realized. Something unfeigned and completely natural, the very opposite of what you'd expect a famous movie star to be like.

And for the first time, Zach maybe understood what had made her a star—a *true* star, not some flash-in-the-pan reality show personality. Because Mallory Keyes was genuine. Real. *Whole*. A woman who held nothing back. And had that something that made it impossible to look away when she was on-screen. Even if that screen was only his forty-two-inch TV.

Because, yeah, Netflix.

Then she looked up and saw him standing there, and that dimpled smile, the mischievous spark in her eyes, damn near stopped his heart.

Only this time, he knew better than to pay any of it any mind.

This time, he was smart enough to avoid complications. To avoid *her*.

Which he more or less managed for the rest of the evening. Not her presence, obviously—small house and all that—but anything resembling real conversation? You bet.

Except it wasn't as if he couldn't hear her low laugh, or notice how she'd goof around with her mother…or the way the little ones swarmed her like ants on a sugar cube. How easily and often she'd send the older two into gleeful shrieking by making the goofiest faces he'd ever seen a grown woman make.

Still, Zach remained in control, resolved not to let any of it get to him. To not let Mallory get to him, simply because she was pretty and had a great laugh and could reduce his kids into giggling puddles. Until, a couple hours later, he found her in his parents' dimly lit living room, his youngest child sacked out against her chest, her cheek resting in his curls, and his heart nearly stopped all over again.

Hell.

Chapter Six

Sensing Zach's presence behind her, Mallory silently sighed, gently stirring Liam's red curls under her chin. And only partly because Zach's arrival meant giving up this precious bundle in her arms.

"I suppose you want your child back now," she whispered.

"It is getting late," Zach whispered back, his boots softly scraping against the worn wood floors in the cozy little room before he sank into an old leather recliner across from her. "Val and my brother already left with their two."

"Oh! I'm sorry I didn't get to say goodbye."

She could barely see him in the scant light eking from the hallway, but the slump to his shoulders as he sat forward in the chair made her heart ache. Especially since she figured his obvious exhaustion wasn't only physical. "Val knew you were in here with Liam. She said not to bother you, she'll catch you later." He paused. "I can tell, she really likes you."

"The feeling's mutual." In fact, it was almost startling, how quickly she and Val had become friends. Almost as easily as Zach's mother and hers, chattering away in the kitchen. Her intuition had been dead-on, that Mama needed more human interaction than only hanging out with her daughter 24/7. Could be why she'd taken poor little Edgar to the vet so often, simply to get out of the house. What Mallory hadn't realized, though, was that Mama wasn't the only one craving companionship, that maybe Mallory wasn't as much of a hermit as she'd thought. Then she thought she heard Zach chuckle.

"I don't blame you for hiding out, though. We definitely get a little loud when we're all together."

Zach excepted, Mallory thought, even as she pushed out a little laugh. "Okay, you got me. Don't get me wrong, I love people. And your family…they're great. Really. It's been a long time since I enjoyed myself that much. But I've never been much for parties."

"Not even fancy Hollywood ones?"

"Especially those. Well, except maybe for getting to dress up. That was fun. But it's one thing to be 'on' when you're in front of the camera, another thing entirely when you're not. One of the things I do not miss, believe me. Since I'm one of those people who needs to recharge every couple of hours. For both my sake and everyone's around me." She looked around. "So this is the house Granville Blake gave your folks after your dad retired?"

She heard Zach release a breath, as though grateful for the subject change. "Yeah. It's small, but adequate. Mom's not much of a decorator, but she as least added some color to it. Lots of this stuff clients gave her over the years. And she finds a perfect spot for every gift."

"I can tell. It's adorable. And very homey. In fact, it

gives me some ideas for my own place, see if I can make it feel more…welcoming." The little one stirred in her lap; she raked her hand through his silky curls. "Did he get this red hair from his mother?"

A second's hesitation preceded, "Hers was darker. More…auburn, I guess. Her grandmother had the really red hair." He smiled. "Good Irish stock. What about you? Or is that…?"

"My true color? It was at one time. Now it has help. And don't look too closely, I haven't had a chance yet to find a decent local colorist. If there is such a thing."

His mouth twitched. "I wouldn't've pegged you to care about stuff like that."

"You've met my mother, what do you think?" she said, and he smiled, then nodded toward the toddler. "How on earth did that happen?"

Mallory angled her head to look down at that angelic little face, smeared with barbecue sauce and ice cream. His mouth open, he released a shuddering little sigh and sagged back into sleep, and her chest cramped. "He wanted a ride on the 'car chair,' he called it. So I obliged. I'd forgotten how quickly little kids can pass out, though. One minute we were having quite the conversation and the next—silence."

"I'm sorry, the kid weighs a ton—"

"I can't really feel him, Zach," she said gently. "Not on my legs, anyway."

"Oh. Right. Sorry."

"No worries, I'm used to—"

"Idiots being insensitive?"

"You're hardly insensitive. And you're definitely not an idiot. And anyway, most people aren't that way on purpose. They simply don't know. I sure didn't before it happened to me. In any case, I don't take offense very easily." She paused. "Except when I get the feeling someone's deliberately avoiding me." Even in the dark, she could see his eyes dart to hers. "Did you think I wouldn't notice?"

One side of his mouth ticked up. "It wasn't personal."

"The hell you say."

At least he laughed before he sighed. "I guess I felt a little blindsided. Since I didn't know you were coming."

"You're kidding. I assumed Val told you."

He shook his head. "Although I did wonder why dinner had been moved here."

"She said she has too many stairs. But I don't understand. What was there to be blindsided about?"

Zach reached up to fiddle with his glasses, then leaned forward, his hands clasped together. "Like I said, it wasn't you. It's just...well. I probably said more than I should have. Earlier, I mean. At lunch?"

Honestly, what was it with men being so damned afraid of coming across as vulnerable? As *human*, for heaven's sake? "Please don't tell me you were embarrassed."

"Not embarrassed as much as...unnerved."

No surprise there. "Because?"

"I'm not much of a sharer. Not generally, anyway."

She smiled. "Not even with your wife?"

A beat or two preceded, "The one exception."

That didn't surprise her, either. "And somehow that all added up to you deciding to give me a wide berth."

He pushed out a sound that was half sigh, half laugh. "I guess it doesn't make a whole lot of sense, does it?"

"Not from where I'm sitting, no. Although what it sounded like to me, was that you've been carting some of that stuff around inside your head for a long time. It needed to be set free."

After a moment, he nodded. "You sound like you've been there."

"Takes one to know one," she said on a breath. "Because expectations are a real pain in the butt."

"Whose?"

"Does it matter? Our own, other people's...the result's the same. We get so caught up in what we think we're supposed to be, how we're supposed to act, that we ignore how we *are*. That what we're really feeling isn't valid, you know? Good or bad."

"Or we don't want everyone else to worry."

"Exactly." The little one stirred, then sat up, blinked at Mallory with a crumpled brow like he couldn't for the life of him figure out who she was or how he'd gotten there, then reached for his daddy, his lower lip quivering. Chuckling, Zach stood and hiked his son into his arms, his protectiveness so potent it practically bounced off the small room's walls. "It's also one of the few things we feel we have control over," Mallory said, folding her arms over the sudden chill left in the child's wake.

Molding the little cutie to his chest and cupping his head, Zach looked at her for a long moment. "Is control such a bad thing?"

She wasn't sure if the question was rhetorical or not, but she answered anyway. "It is if it keeps us from living a genuine life. Don't you think? Especially if it's only another word for *fear*—"

"Dad? Where are you?"

"Be there in a sec," Zach yelled back to Jeremy, then frowned at Mallory for another couple of seconds before finally saying, "You up for a little ride tomorrow morning?"

She actually jerked. "With you?"

"Yes, with me. I've got an appointment someplace I think you might be interested in seeing."

"Where?"

"Like I'd give you a chance to say no?"

"That sounds ominous."

"Guess you'll just have to trust me, won't you?"

There was something almost playful in his voice. Something warm and kind and…and challenging. A far different sort of challenge to the ones she was used to facing, she suspected, although no less scary in its own way. But yes, she trusted him. Even if she wasn't sure she trusted herself.

"What time will you pick me up?" she said, and he grinned.

Zach wasn't entirely sure what'd come over him the night before. Except hearing the gentle challenge in her voice, about figuring out the difference between control and fear, about living a genuine life…it occurred to him maybe the woman could use a dose of her own medicine. Why he should be the one to administer it, he hadn't wholly figured out yet. Except Heidi had been big on looking for ways to make the world a better place, one day at a time, one person at a time. The same philosophy he'd grown up with, actually, but it wasn't until he fell in love with the world's most enthusiastic proponent of that mind-set that it finally got through that making someone else happy was the only way to be truly happy yourself.

An area of his life he'd sorely neglected of late.

Of course, it was highly possible his plan could blow up in his face, that Mallory would say, "Oh, hell, no," and wheel herself into the next county.

"You've brought me to another ranch?" she said as they drove up to the Flying Star, not ten miles from the Colorado border.

No, he hadn't come clean yet. Although he could tell it'd been driving her nuts that he hadn't. Despite that— not to mention how her musky, floral scent had slapped his senses silly when he'd lifted her out of the wheelchair to set her in the passenger seat of his truck—conversation had been easy enough, on the drive up. Clearly she did trust him, which was equal parts gratifying and terrifying. Yes, even though he'd gotten himself into this mess all by himself. She had a million questions, it seemed, about the area, the town. Not the touristy stuff, which she already knew, but what made its heart beat, she said. What made people call it home.

In answer, Zach had pointed out the windshield toward the landscape, the vibrant fall sky, and she'd slowly nodded, her smile saying she understood.

"It's so...real."

"Yeah," he'd said.

"But it's more about the people, isn't it?"

He'd smirked. "Don't kid yourself. We're not perfect."

"Exactly," she'd sighed out, like this was a huge relief.

She'd also talked a lot about Landon—and to the kid, actually, since he'd called while they were driving. She'd even turned her phone around to introduce him to Zach— Edgar's vet and their new friend, she'd said. Good enough, he'd decided. Safe, anyway.

"So where are you two going?" Landon had asked. Zach decided the kid must resemble his father more than Mallory, although in the tiny phone he'd only gotten a glimpse of wild dark hair.

"I don't really know, Zach won't tell me."

"Mom. Really?"

"See what you have to look forward to?" she'd said to Zach, only to then laugh and ask how his father was, and the conversation had devolved into the sweetly mundane, a comfortingly ordinary exchange between a mother and son who clearly adored each other. And Zach's chest had fisted, both because it was obvious the separation sucked for both of them, logic be damned, and because he got to thinking what it would've been like, had Heidi lived—

"It's not just 'another ranch,' exactly," he now said, cutting the engine in front of the main house as he cut off his thoughts. Then he turned to Mallory, his gut doing a quick flip at the puzzled, but amused, look in those clear gray eyes. Because she was real, too. Although not in the least mundane. Or comforting. He looked back at the house. "Think of this as…an opportunity."

"To…?"

"Take the next step in being that example to Landon."

He met her gaze again to find her somehow frowning and smiling simultaneously, although by this time, Adrienne and Booth Edison, the facility's owners, had come out to the truck to meet them, and Mallory looked toward them.

And released a soft "Oh…"

Probably because Adrienne also used a wheelchair.

Around his mother's age, Zach supposed, Adrienne greeted them both with her customary huge smile, waiting patiently while Zach retrieved Mallory's chair and got her settled into it. She did everything but huff her annoyance, though, at having to accept his help. Adrienne chuckled.

"Honey, a word of advice—when you get the chance to get a good-lookin' man's arms around you, take it!"

"Yeah," her husband said, "I kinda figured you weren't nearly as helpless as you make out to be."

"You got that right. So." Adrienne looked back at Mallory. "You ready?"

She glanced up at Zach, then back at Adrienne. "I'm not entirely sure what I'm supposed to be ready for."

The graying brunette gave Zach an admonishing look. "You didn't tell her?"

"You all came out before I had the chance."

"Which I suppose you never got in the forty minutes it took you to get up here," Adrienne said, then turned to Mallory. "Men. Well, come on, Henry's waiting. You may as well come, too, Zachary, since this was your idea. And no, Booth, the mare can wait, she ain't gonna foal in the next twenty minutes."

* * *

Of course by the time they reached the ranch Mallory had an inkling about what Zach had up his sleeve. What she hadn't yet decided was whether to be touched by the gesture or throttle the man. As if she could do such a thing. But even if she hadn't figured out what was afoot, the long ramps inside the squeaky-clean, metal-walled barn would've given it away. As though sensing they needed space, Adrienne hung back, talking quietly with Henry. Or maybe Henry was the handsome, and very placid, chestnut gelding standing at the far end of the ramp. All saddled up. Waiting.

For her.

"You want me to get on a horse." Her voice echoed in the cavernous space, the slight echo taunting. Chiding.

"Think of it more as…several things falling into place. What you said the other day, then last night. Then your mother reminding me about how you haven't ridden since your accident—"

"So this is her idea?"

"No, ma'am, entirely mine. And it didn't even occur to me until I remembered the appointment this morning. But this isn't about me, or her, or anybody wanting you to do anything. It's about…"

He squatted beside her, a move that under normal circumstances would've irritated the snot out of her—as though she were a child who needed to be cajoled into doing something she didn't want to do. And she wasn't entirely sure that wasn't the case here.

His smile would be her undoing. "Like I said, I'm only giving you an opportunity. The rest is up to you. If it puts your mind at ease, though, this is what Adrienne does full-time."

The horse shifted slightly, as though impatient for her

to get on with it. Of course she knew that wasn't true, that therapy horses were the very epitomes of patience—

"I'm scared," she said, so softly she could barely hear her own voice.

"I know."

Zach didn't touch her, didn't try to reassure her or talk her out of her feelings. Didn't even ask her to explain them. All he did was give her permission to feel them.

Something nobody else had ever done.

Mallory shut her eyes, thinking how rah-rah everyone else had been since the accident, pushing her forward, never letting her give up, never giving her even a moment to doubt herself. Sometimes they'd meant well—like Mama— other times it was because helplessness makes other people uncomfortable. Her ex, for example. But whatever their motives, the result had been the same: A lot more of her so-called progress than she'd realized had been for others' benefit than her own.

"I can really leave if I want to?"

Zach stood, his hands on his hips. "You really can."

Such a heady thing, freedom.

She grasped the wheels' rims. Breathed in, out. In, out. Felt Zach's touch on her shoulder, light and firm and steady. Then Adrienne rolled up next to her.

"Zach tells me you were a barrel racer."

"I was. Once upon a time."

"You must miss it."

Almost the same words Zach had used when asking her about her acting career. Her reaction, though, couldn't've been more different. Because this time, heat surged through her. Of remembered adrenaline rushes. Joy. That freedom thing again.

Her heart started beating so fast she half thought she might pass out. "I do."

"For me," Adrienne said, "it was being afraid of not

being able to feel the horse under me. Of not having the control I'd been so proud of. Finally realized nobody else was gonna get past that for me. *But* me."

Mallory turned to the older woman. "How long before you got back on?"

Adrienne's lips tilted, like she understood. "Six months. And don't go comparing yourself to me or anybody else," she said, when Mallory looked back at the horse, frowning. "Everyone's path is different."

"And some are shorter than others."

"This is very true."

Zach squeezed her shoulder. "Would it be easier if I left?"

"Probably. But I don't want you to."

Adrienne chuckled. "You saying what I think you're saying?"

"God help me, but…okay." She gripped the rims again. "Let's do this."

She had a choice of using a harness and crane to be set on the horse, or—as Adrienne suggested—rolling up the ramp into a closer position so she could grab the horn and hoist herself over the saddle, which was specially fitted with a back brace and various belts to strap her in and wrap around her thighs.

"There's as many ways of getting on and off a horse as there are people. It might take some trial and error to figure out which method works best for you. We can even help you train a horse to kneel so you get on, if that's a method that appeals. You get in and out of a car by yourself? Without a lift, I mean?"

"Yeah, actually."

"Then you should be able to do this."

Mallory nodded toward the horse. "Could he and I have a little chat first?"

"Sure thing. Henry?" The horse's ears flicked. "Got somebody for you to meet."

The horse calmly eyed her as she rolled up to him, lowering his head so she could finger his bridle's nose-band, inhale the intoxicating aroma of leather and horse. Maybe the scent seemed stronger because they were in-side, or maybe because anticipation had heightened her senses, but it'd been a long time since she'd felt this... ready. For anything.

"Are we cool, dude?" she whispered, gently stroking his blaze. "Because I have no idea what I'm doing..."

Then she looked over at Zach, still there, his thumbs hooked in his jeans' pockets, his mouth canted in that sorta smile that had already become endearingly familiar. And frighteningly dear.

"Okay," she said. "Let's do this."

Zach moved in to hold the bridle, an unnecessary pre-caution since Henry was the calmest horse in the universe. Still, it felt good knowing he was there, that he wouldn't let her topple off the animal, even if he couldn't prevent her looking like an idiot as, with Booth's help, she finally got herself in the damn saddle.

But once she was...

"Oh, my goodness," she breathed out, realizing she was grinning like a fool.

Zach laughed. "How's it feel?"

"Incredible." She looked down at Adrienne. "Can I take him out?"

"If you want, sure. Wouldn't try anything too fancy, though—"

"I won't." She reached out to pat the horse's neck, then wrapped the reins around her hand, the familiarity of the simple gesture sending a thrill of pleasure through her. "I promise." Her gaze met Zach's. "You'll come with me?"

There went that smile again. Only this time she saw

a spark in his eyes she hadn't before. If pressed, she'd have to say the man was tickled pink with himself, that his plan had worked. Which in turn ignited in Mallory a spark of another sort, one she hadn't felt in longer than she could remember:

Competitiveness.

"You have to ask?" Zach said, and she thought, *Oh, yeah, buddy...the game is on.* Not that she knew when, or how, she'd get even, but get even, she would.

Because she was a real big believer in the Golden Rule.

"What're you grinning about?" Zach asked, a lightness buoying his words that made her heart sing and ache at the same time. She glanced down at him, at this dear, kind man who deserved a good, swift kick in the rear to blast him out of the hole he seemed determined to bury himself in.

"That right in this moment," she said, looking in front of her, "things couldn't be better." When she lowered her gaze again, he was facing forward, his expression...careful, she thought. "Thank you."

A smile flickered. "You're welcome. But it was no big deal."

"For you, maybe," she said after a moment. "For me? Hell, yes."

His quiet laugh wrapped right around her heart and squeezed tight.

It was a careful ride, for sure, this first venture back into that world she'd loved more than anything for so long. But every bit as thrilling as the first time she'd felt the power of a horse galloping underneath her, her first rodeo, her first win. She couldn't feel her legs, no, but somehow Henry became her legs. And she'd never felt more free.

It was over too soon, but everyone agreed she probably shouldn't push too hard, too fast. She knew they were right, but...

"When can I come back?" she said later in Adrienne's kitchen after the woman made her a cup of tea and Zach had finally gone to check on that mare. Weathered skin pleated at the corners of the woman's deep brown eyes.

"Once a horse junkie, always a horse junkie. But if you're really serious, you should probably think about getting your own horse. So the two of you can train together." The other woman took a sip of her own tea. "Zach said you already bought a horse for your son."

"I did. Although I haven't brought him over yet. I suppose it'd crossed my mind, how great it would be to be able to ride with Landon, but…" She smiled. "Now I can. Or at least eventually."

"He's coming out soon, I take it?"

"Yes. End of next week, in fact." Then she frowned. "How'd you know that…? Wait—what's Zach said?"

A funny little smile curved the woman's mouth. "Enough to know the boy's sweet on you."

"Hardly," Mallory mumbled, even as her cheeks burned. Adrienne leaned forward.

"I'm not saying he knows that yet. Or to be honest if he'll ever figure it out. Men can be dumb as bricks sometimes. And the way he loved his wife…" Humor sparkled in her eyes. "I used to tell Booth, he needed to take lessons."

"So you've known Zach for a while?"

"All his life. Horse people from the same area are like family. Which I suppose you know all too well, growing up in a ranching community yourself."

Mallory almost laughed. "What else did he tell you?"

"Well, let's see…that you're divorced and your boy lives with his daddy back in LA, that *you* live with your mama and a spoiled Boston terrier named Edward—"

"Edgar."

"Edgar, right. And that you're a film star. Although he

didn't have to tell me that part, I already knew it. What he didn't tell me was that you're even prettier in person than you are on-screen. But I suspect he'd decided to keep that part to himself. So I wouldn't jump to any conclusions he didn't want me jumping to. Only, in my experience? Men don't generally talk that much about a gal they're not interested in."

A huge, fluffy gray cat jumped up onto Mallory's lap and settled in, purring loudly enough to rattle windows. Smiling, Mallory began stroking the soft fur, then said, "So, tell me your story. What happened?"

Adrienne snorted. "That wouldn't be you changing the subject, now, would it?"

"Absolutely. Well?"

"Car accident, twenty years ago," the other woman said flatly. "That I wasn't killed was a damn miracle. Like you, I was heavy into the rodeo life. Couldn't imagine doing anything else. However in those days there weren't as many options as there are now. Or at least, people didn't think so. I got back up on a horse, absolutely. But I never competed again."

"You still ride?"

"Some. But my injury…" The older woman's mouth thinned. "I was grateful for what I had. What I could still do. What I *can* still do. But I finally decided maybe I needed to focus my energies elsewhere. So Booth and I set up this place." She swept a graying strand of wavy dark hair behind her ear, revealing a small diamond stud. "We don't only work with spinal cord injuries, but with all kinds of folks who could benefit from what the horses have to offer. Something about them…they're just natural healers, you know?"

"I do," Mallory said. She'd seen it before, of course, when she was younger, even if she'd temporarily forgotten—that almost magical way horses often had of making a person connect with something inside themselves they hadn't even known was there. How almost angel-like they were, in a way—four-legged, hooved emissaries of joy. Of power. How working with them, riding them, required a combination of control and trust that inspired, *instilled*, confidence and freedom—

"What're you thinking?" Adrienne asked, and Mallory released a breath.

"How funny it is, the way life works. That I'd given up—willingly—such a huge part of who I was to go in an entirely different direction. Only to be led right back to the beginning, maybe." She met Adrienne's astute gaze. "I guess I always thought of life as linear. Maybe not so much?"

The other woman leaned back in her chair, her hands folded over the stomach. "Guess that depends on what we have to learn, whether or not we keep moving forward or circle back for a refresher course on what we might've missed before." Then she released a deep belly laugh that made Mallory smile. "As good a philosophy as any, I suppose."

Her husband and Zach reappeared a moment later. After a couple minutes' conversation about the expectant mare—everything looked good, Zach doubted they'd need him for the foaling—Mallory and Zach were back on the road, both lost in thought as they listened to whatever country station they could pick up out this far. And why did it not surprise her that Zach Talbot would be so old-school? It was kind of comforting, in a way, reminding her of that road-trip movie she'd done a few years back, the one set in the sixties. That character, too, had not been the same person at the end of the story she'd been at the beginning, same as the woman returning to Whispering Pines was most definitely not the same one who'd left this morning.

"When I said I was scared," she finally said, "how come you didn't press the issue? Ask for details?"

A moment passed before he said, his gaze fixed out the windshield, "Because I figured the details didn't matter." His gaze barely bounced off hers. "Did they?"

"Not really, I guess."

"Then there ya go. And anyway, this wasn't about me. The *why* behind whatever that fear was...didn't figure it was any of my business."

"I see."

She heard him blow out a short breath. "I'm not trying to shut you out, Mallory. Believe it or not. You wanna talk, I'll listen. Like I said. But I figure the stuff inside a person's head is private, you know? More than that...it's, well, *sacred*, I guess you could call it. Nobody has any right to go poking around in there unless they'd been specifically invited. So my only goal was to see you happy. And I'm guessing you were."

"Still am," she said softly, then glanced at Zach's profile, his expression so set—his smile so careful when his gaze shot to hers—she got the distinct feeling he wasn't the only one who'd gone through some changes that morning. Only no way in hell was she gonna open *that* can of worms. Or, as he said, go poking around someplace she hadn't been invited.

Because why ruin a perfect day?

Chapter Seven

A week later, Zach still couldn't shake the memory of the look on Mallory's face when she'd finally gotten on Henry, a look that shot right past joy to absolute triumph. Only thing to equal it had been Heidi's expression, right after she'd given birth to the boys. That Zach had been in some way the cause of both had unnerved him far more than he was about to let on.

"Here you go, guys!" At Levi's bellow, Zach looked up to see his taller, brawnier brother navigating the crowd in the bleachers, one large hand clamped around an open cardboard box piled high with hot dogs and nachos and cotton candy, the other precariously balancing another box jammed with cans of soda. The nippy fall air smelled of animal and dung, sawdust and fried food, the afternoon sun still high in a bright blue sky. Forget the thrill of competition, Zach thought, barely able to keep the boys from attacking their uncle like baby wolves. Never mind the breath-holding anticipation of how long the cowboy could stay on the bull, or whether the clowns could keep the bull distracted long enough for said cowboy to save his ass. For these two, it was all about the food.

It was always about the food.

A few feet away, Val laughed, her lap full of baby Risa, her eyes full of happy. "Good God, Zach—when was the last time you fed them?"

"An hour ago?" he said, watching the boys inhale their hot dogs, and the blonde laughed again. You would've never known the wedding was only two days out. Lord, Heidi had been an absolute basket case. Then again, they'd done the whole church-wedding-and-reception-for-a-hundred deal—mostly for Heidi's relatives and family friends he'd never seen before. Or since. Frankly, it'd been beyond him why most of 'em had even bothered coming. And after her mother'd moved out to Phoenix after Heidi's father died a few months after Heidi, the boys only saw her two, three times a year. So no way would he take them away from their other grandparents. Especially after the scare with his father—

"Hey," Levi said, nudging Zach with his elbow. "Isn't that Mallory and her mother down there?"

The handicapped-accessible area wasn't huge—but then again, neither was the venue. They were also sitting maybe twenty feet away…which made it ridiculously easy for even Jeremy's squeaky, high-pitched "Mallory!" to reach her ears.

She and her mother both turned, Mallory shielding her eyes in the bright sunshine. Which had turned her hair the color of lust. Not that Zach had ever thought of lust being a color until now. Until Mallory Keyes and her damn hair.

"Up here!" Val yelled, waving madly, and half the people below them twisted around to look up. For such a tiny person, Levi's almost-wife had lungs on her like a moose. Mallory smiled and waved back and that lust thing got a whole lot worse. At least, that's what Zach was going with. Because that, he could deal with. That, he could handle. That, he could dismiss simply as a whackadoo reaction to loneliness and grief and an epic case of it'd-been-too-long. Rather than, say, an actual attraction to the woman whose hair had provoked the whackadoo reaction. Because…no.

"Can we go see 'em?" Jeremy asked, already halfway on the next riser, never mind the burly cowboy in his way. And of course Liam, sensing adventure, was not about to be left out.

"Me, too?"

"Yeah," Jeremy said, licking cotton candy from his fingers and adding streaks of putrid pink to bilious yellow mustard smears all over his face. "Maybe her mother has cookies."

Zach gawked at his oldest, wondering not for the first time how his brain worked, only to hear Levi chuckle and say, "Kid has a point. What? You never know."

In any case, he could hardly ignore any of it. His kids, her hair, Levi's grin. So he took two very sticky hands in his own and navigated the sea of butts and backs until he reached ground level, where Mallory hauled Liam up into her lap and her smile knocked him clear to Colorado.

"I figured y'all would be here somewhere!" she said, tugging the toddler closer and making him giggle.

"You probably should've hosed him down before you did that."

"Please. For years Landon's favorite thing to wear was mud. And everything I've got on is old as the hills." Jeans. Boots. A blazer over a sweater. Nothing special. And yet…

"So it's all good. Right, bud?" she said, giving Liam another squeeze.

"Yeah," Liam said, settling in against Mallory's chest and making Zach's ache.

"Excuse me," said a beefy cowboy, glaring at Mallory

in her wheelchair. Even though she wasn't in the way at all, it was the rest of them—

"I'm so sorry," she said, "we're causing a real traffic jam, aren't we? Mama, scoot down so they can sit—"

"That's okay," Zach said, "we only came to say hi—"

"Did you bring cookies?" Jeremy asked, wiggling his little butt onto the riser beside Dorelle. Who burst out laughing.

"Now why would I do that," she said, "when there's so many goodies to eat here? Which, judging from this mess—" Her brightly patterned wrap slipped off one shoulder as reached into her purse for a tissue to wipe the boy's face. Instead, shreds of tissue clung to the cotton candy residue. Still chuckling, she tried to pluck off the tufts, tucking them into the palm of her hand. And Jeremy actually *let her.* "—you've already sampled."

Sighing, Zach sat on the riser by Mallory, then reached for Liam. But the little boy shook his head, twisting to look up at her, his expression rapturous. "You smell good."

"Why, thank you, sweetie," she said, wrapping her arms more tightly around him to whisper, "So do you."

"I do?"

"Oh, yes. Like cotton candy and hot dogs. Yum. In fact," she teased, as she lowering her mouth to his temple, "I could just eat you up..." Then she made gobbly monster sounds that sent Liam into gales of laughter...and Zach over the edge of something he hadn't known was there, into something that scared the hell out of him.

Even as his little boy's infectious giggles made him laugh, too.

The wind picked up from the east, making Mallory's hair tumble across her face as the chute opened and a small herd of cows surged into the arena.

"I take it Josh'll be up soon?" she asked, digging into the purse tucked beside her hip for a clip of some kind.

Carefully balancing Liam on her lap, she quickly twisted up the tangled mass and clamped it into place with a natural grace Zach found completely mesmerizing.

"Uh, yeah," Zach said. "In fact…"

The crowd murmured as his brother entered the arena on Thor, easily the best cutter in the state. As four other riders positioned themselves to keep things in check, Josh and Thor calmly moved as one into the center of the herd, efficiently separating an all-white steer from the group. Then came the dance—the cow determined to rejoin his buddies, horse and rider equally determined that not happen, the horse's graceful, lightning-quick zigzags frustrating the cow. Two and a half minutes later, Josh had cut his two cows without breaking a sweat and waved to his adoring crowd with a grin.

Hugging Liam closer as a cloud of peach-colored dust washed over them, Mallory chuckled. "He's really full of himself, isn't he?"

"From the time he could walk. Although at least he has reason."

"Very true. I had him bring Waffles over yesterday, by the way."

"Oh, yeah?"

"Yeah," she blew out, then rested her cheek on Liam's head as she looked over, her eyes silvery-soft. "I found a ramp online that'd be perfect for me to mount him from my wheelchair, if he'll let me. You put it together like a kid's building set. Well, *I* can't put it together, but somebody can. It'll be here in a few days. So, see what you did?" Releasing a breath, she looked back over the arena. "Of course, now I need a second horse so Landon and I can ride together."

Zach smiled. "He is gonna be so proud of you."

"What makes you say that?"

"Because I can tell how much he loves you. He's a good kid."

Softly laughing, Mallory smoothed Liam's curls away from her mouth. "You reached this conclusion from talking to him for, what? Thirty seconds?"

"You forget I could overhear the two of you the whole rest of the time. So…am I wrong?"

"That he's a good kid? No, but…"

"Then there ya go."

Zach thought she blushed, but that might've been the wind on her cheeks. "Thanks."

"It wasn't a stretch, considering who his mother is."

This time, the laugh was sharper. "And you do realize that sounded suspiciously like a line?"

"Right. Because the perfect place to, ah…" he glanced at Liam, intent on watching the next competitor "…do that is in a crowd. With my child on the woman's lap, no less."

Mallory slid a sly grin his way, and his stomach jerked. "Whatever works, right?"

"And would it have? Under other circumstances, I mean?"

What the hell?

He couldn't look at her. He could, however, feel her gaze on the side of his face. Felt it just as intensely when she looked away.

"Who says it didn't?" she said so softly he wasn't sure he heard right. Liam wriggled off Mallory's lap and moved closer to Dorelle, apparently figuring more interesting stuff was going on over where his brother was. Several more seconds of silence—between them, anyway, since the arena was like a rock concert—passed before she asked, "Were we…flirting?"

"Beats me," Zach said. "It's been so long I'm not sure I remember how."

"God's truth," she said, sighing. Then she smiled, not

looking at him. "We probably shouldn't do that again. You know, because of those circumstances and all."

"Right."

"Although—speaking only for myself—it felt good." Her gaze briefly touched his. "To flirt. To feel like…"

"I know. And yeah, it did. Except—"

"No, got it, really. But for a moment, you made me feel like a woman. Not just a woman in a wheelchair. That was nice."

Zach's throat got so tight he could barely swallow his spit. He remembered what she'd said about her husband, wondered about all the things she hadn't. Whether he should or not. Besides that, though, for a moment he'd also felt like something more than…whatever he was these days. To admit that, however, would only be courting disaster. On many levels. So all he said was, "Glad to be of service, then," and she laughed again.

God, he loved that laugh. Then she looked around, taking in the crowd. Such as it was.

"This brings back so many memories," she said. "First rodeo my daddy took me to was about this size, when I was so little he had to put me on his shoulders so I could see. Dinky little local thing. Even smaller than this. The junior high competition I entered a few years later seemed huge by comparison. Then high school after that."

"How'd you do?"

A moment of silence preceded, "High School National champion in barrels at sixteen."

"Get out."

One side of her mouth lifted. "Now you know my secret."

"You ever go pro?"

"Never got the chance," she said on a sigh. "Since I left for Hollywood soon as I graduated from high school." Not looking at him, she picked up a can of soda from the edge of the bench and took a long pull from the straw. "Josh said he doesn't compete much anymore, either."

"No. But he earned more than a few real pretty belt buckles for what you just witnessed. Did the State Fair down in Albuquerque a few times."

"So the Vista wasn't always only a horse breeding operation?"

"Recent development. When we were kids it was a working mama-and-calf operation. There's still a small, rotating herd of heifers for Josh to train with, but that's about it."

"Why'd it change?"

"I'm guessing it got to be more than Granville felt he could handle. Or wanted to deal with. Although he hasn't sold off any of the acreage yet. Not sure what his plans are on that score. There's a handful of hunting lodges on the land, too, so lots of possibilities there."

Looking away, Mallory balanced the cup on one knee. "It's a gorgeous property. Probably worth a fortune."

"Maybe. But not my area of expertise. Or interest."

"So you don't see yourself becoming a rancher, huh?"

"No, ma'am. I'm perfectly happy doing what I'm doing."

His face warmed under her gentle scrutiny. "I can see that." Then she turned away again. "Seems a shame, though, your brother putting so much energy into something that's not even his."

And there it was again, that empathy that twisted him all up inside. "Josh is young yet. Plenty of time to work toward establishing his own operation. Right now his first priority—after his son, of course, since Austin's mom took off when he was a baby—is to Granville and the Vista."

"Because Granville's sick, you mean."

"Yeah," Zach said on a breath. "And we all owe the old man a lot. He's been…" He swallowed. "He's always been real good to us. All of us. Looking out for him now...it's the least we can do."

A beat passed before she said, "The Talbots are a very loyal bunch, aren't they?"

"It's that small-town survival thing—"

"No, I think it's more than that with y'all." Her gaze shifted back to his. "It's simply who you are. You're good people. Genuinely good, I mean. People who keep your promises."

"Our parents would tan our hides if we didn't. So," he said, changing the subject, "you looking forward to teaching Landon to ride?"

She picked up the soda again, taking another long swallow before saying, "Not sure I can, actually. Give him instructions, sure. Catch him if he falls off? Not so much."

"Even though you know the chance of that is pretty slim."

"Yeah, well," she said quietly, "stuff happens."

Right. Like breaking your back in a skiing accident. Or a car skidding on a random patch of ice—

"What about your mother?" he said.

"She never rode. Never mind there's no way she could catch eighty pounds of flailing eleven-year-old. But it's okay, I've got some time yet to figure it out—"

"Hey, guys!" In a flutter of long blond hair, Val appeared with a wriggly one-year-old in her arms. Propping one hand on Zach's shoulder, she lowered herself to the ground in front of Mallory, only to wobble precariously when Risa suddenly lurched to one side. Zach reached for the kid before she landed on her noggin, getting a drooly grin for his efforts. From the baby, not Val.

"Honestly, you little monkey," she said, cupping the baby's dark curls, then turned back to Mallory. "Levi and I were wondering if you and your mama would like to come to the wedding tomorrow out at the Vista?"

"I don't... What?"

"I know it's last minute and all, but half the town will be there, anyway, probably. And between Gus and AJ and Annie there's gonna be enough food to feed the five thousand." Then she turned to Zach and winked. "And anyway, this dude needs a date."

"Excuse me?"

"Hey, Dorelle," Val called over, ignoring him. "Wanna come to our wedding?"

Mallory's mother sucked in a breath like she'd been invited to Buckingham Palace. "Ohmigosh, I'd be honored. What can I bring?"

"Absolutely nothing," Val said, reclaiming her babbling daughter. "So that's settled then. You don't have to dress up or anything, I imagine most people'll be in jeans, anyway. And no gifts, you hear? It's at three, but you can get there pretty much any time after two..."

Then she started back up to her fiancé and older daughter, stopping to chat with at least a half dozen people on her way. Mallory pushed out a little laugh. "She's like a sudden storm, isn't she?"

"These days? For sure."

"You ever notice how contagious other people's happiness is?"

"Is it?"

"It is if you let it be."

He thought about that for a second. "I suppose. Still. You don't have to come if you don't want to."

"And leave my mother to her own devices with a bunch of handsome cowboys? Not a chance. Besides, Val's right—you do need a date."

His mouth open to protest, Zach looked over to see amusement flashing in her eyes, and achingly vivid memories exploded behind his. Of sweet times, happy times, now lost forever except in his memory. But filtered through those memories was something else, something equally achy if not quite as sweet, filmed over with about a million layers of guilt:

Need.

His gaze drifted to Mallory's mouth, a mouth he suddenly wanted to taste so badly it made him a little dizzy. He thought of how they'd flirted earlier, with temptation, with possibilities, with things barely acknowledged before they'd shoved them back into whatever deep, dark hole they'd popped out of—

"Daddy?" He looked to see Liam standing beside him, shivering so hard he was blurred. "I'm c-cold." Zach instantly shrugged off his jacket to wrap it around the little guy, but judging from the kid's blue lips they were done here.

"Wanna go home?" Zach said, hauling the kid into his arms as he stood.

He let out a wobbly yawn. "Uh-huh."

"Aw, poor little guy," Mallory said, reaching for Liam's hand, prompting a brief, quivering smile in return. "I'm guessing nap time?"

"Only three-year-old in the world who still takes 'em."

"Lucky you. But Jeremy can stay with Mom and me, if he wants."

"Oh. Well, I'm sure Levi and Val—"

"They already left. Yeesh, you guys are dropping like flies. Or at least your kids are."

He looked down at Liam, then back at Mallory. "If you're sure..?"

"Wouldn't've offered if I wasn't. Besides, Mom's in hog heaven, in case you hadn't noticed."

Zach glanced over at Dorelle and Jeremy, deep in conversation about heaven knew what. Ever since he was little, the kid had had a way of zeroing in on people who maybe needed a little extra attention, who were lonely or unhappy or whatever. Like his mama, Zach realized. Zach also remembered those times when he was a kid and the family would have to leave someplace early because Levi and Josh—seven years younger than Zach—had reached their breaking point. And how pissed he'd been at them for ruining his fun. Of course, all was forgiven once he was old enough to drive and could fend for himself. But back then...

"Then thanks," he said to Mallory. "I live right next to the clinic—"

"I know. So go. We'll be fine. But..." Her eyes twinkled. "Is it a date? For your brother's wedding?" She grinned. "Because whatever a bride wants on her wedding day, she should get, right?"

Not a real date, of course. He knew that. As did she. Still. He wondered which of them this was a bigger step for?

"Right. So you want me to pick you up or...?"

"No, it's probably easier if we meet you over there. Around two-thirty?"

"Sounds good," he said, then called to Jeremy, "Liam's cold, I'm taking him home. You okay with staying with Mallory and Dorelle?"

His oldest gave him a thumb's-up—honestly—and Zach hitched Liam higher up in his arms before looking down at Mallory, into those soft gray eyes that would be the death of him. Not to mention the smile barely curving that mouth. And he thought, *Sounds* good? *In what universe?*

Because he'd meant what he'd said, he thought a few minutes later as he punched on the truck's heat and drove his sleepy, freezing little boy home, about never wanting to get sucked in like that, ever again. Not that he didn't love his boys more than his own life, but those were his kids. Loving them wasn't an option, it was simply fact. They were part of him, part of Heidi. All he had left of her. But Heidi had been the only person he'd ever loved that hard.

The only time he'd let down his guard, or acted out of character, or whatever you wanted to call it. Unlike his brothers, who'd all done their fair share of crazy over the years, Zach had always prided himself on his practicality, his ability to weigh the pros and cons of things from a logical perspective before deciding whether or not to act on them. Until Heidi, who'd knocked logic on its ass— or at least, had knocked Zach on his—and he'd fallen so hard and so deep he couldn't've found his way back out if you'd put a gun to his head. He hadn't only been *in* love, he'd been totally and irrevocably *lost* in it. And look what that had cost him.

True, if it hadn't been for all that illogic he wouldn't have the boys, so there was that. And that was a lot. A helluva lot, actually, he mused as he cut the engine in front of his house, then went around the car to scoop a now-sleeping Liam out of his seat, and the little boy slumped heavily against Zach's shoulder, his sticky-sour smell twisting itself around Zach's heart like it always did. He couldn't imagine life without these two. In that way, he was beyond blessed.

But that didn't change the fact that the pain of losing their mother was still there. And always would be. Happiness, he'd learned, came at a heavy price. A far heavier price than he would willingly pay again.

So that flirting business with Mallory earlier…that could not happen again. Wouldn't.

He carried Liam down the hall into the tiny room he shared with his brother, lowering him onto the rumpled toddler bed before covering him with the pathetically worn little lion quilt Heidi had made for Jeremy before he was born. Zach smiled, remembering the tears in Heidi's eyes when four-year-old Jeremy dragged the ratty quilt into their room after Liam was born and tried to stuff it into the bassinet, declaring it was Liam's now. Zach gently fingered the faded patches, the uneven stitching—a lot more love than skill had gone into the thing, but she'd been so proud of it. And he'd been so proud of her—

He slugged his hands into his back pockets, frowning when the image of Mallory seated on Henry's back usurped the one of his wife, the triumph in those gray eyes pushing aside the laughter in Heidi's brown ones, and he thanked God there were no choices to be made, really. That whatever Mallory's reasons for coming here—for hiding—that triumphant moment was a turning point. That if she'd overcome whatever had kept her from doing something she obviously loved so much, it was a pretty safe bet she'd also overcome whatever was keeping her from going home, being with her son full-time.

From finding someone who'd love her the way she deserved to be loved, with no reservations. No fear. Who wouldn't even think twice about surrendering his whole heart and soul to her.

The way he had with Heidi.

In the meantime, he could be her "date" for his brother's wedding, and maybe store up some of that joy for when she wasn't around anymore.

He leaned over to kiss Liam's temple, smiling when the little boy stirred in his sleep. This was his life now.

And it was enough.

"You came!"

The newly minted Mrs. Talbot swooped down on Mallory, giving her a big hug that smelled of white roses and some fruity perfume, the sweet scents pleasantly blending with the tang of burning piñon in the fireplace, the aromas of Mexican spices from the buffet being set out on the other side of the huge room.

Returning the hug, Mallory smiled. "You didn't exactly give me much of choice," she said, and Val straightened, her hands on her hips. She made a breathtaking, if eccentric, bride, in a vintagey, knee-length ivory lace dress and cowboy boots, her gorgeous blond hair painstakingly done up in pearl-studded swirls.

"That was the idea," Val said, grinning.

Mallory grinned back, even though the crowd—so much for a "small" wedding—was beginning to press in on her. This was nothing like the subdued, sophisticated hum of the LA parties she'd grown used to, that was for sure. In fact, the raucous roar of genuine laughter, of kids' gleeful screeching as they zoomed around the room, took her back to her Texas childhood—in itself not a bad thing. But the fact remained that these weren't her people, not really, no matter how welcoming they'd been. It was that thing about small towns again, how hard it was to really become part of something already seamlessly whole and complete.

But she'd also become an expert at living in the moment. So she reached for the bride's hand and gave it a quick squeeze. "You look fantastic."

Val beamed. "Thanks! I was all for wearing jeans, but poor Levi nearly blew a gasket. Said maybe this wasn't my first wedding, but it was his. So this was our compromise. In fact, he picked out the dress. I know, right?" she said when Mallory's mouth fell open. "Of course he nearly blew another gasket when I suggested he might wanna think about moonlighting as a bridal consultant—" A delicate little hiccup popped out of her mouth, which she covered with her hand, giggling. "Sorry. I rarely drink, since I have the alcohol tolerance of a gnat, Levi says." She hiccupped again, then leaned closer. "But day-um, that sparkling wine is so *good*— Oh!"

Levi appeared, tugging his tipsy wife to his side, his

wavy hair and sharp features giving off a definite leading-man vibe. Especially in his dress jeans and boots, the natty sports jacket hanging open over a white Western-style shirt with a silver-and-turquoise bolo tie. The baby girl in his other arm, her dark curls set off by a fetching white floral headband to go with the miniature version of her mama's dress, added an extra touch of adorableness.

"And what are you doing over here all by yourself?" Levi asked Mallory. "Aren't you supposed to be here with my brother?"

Ah, yes. Zach. Who'd fulfilled his duty, or whatever this was, efficiently and politely. Kindly, even. Since Mallory doubted he could be anything less. But with smiles that weren't quite all there and a "Please don't ask why" look in his eyes that of course made her want to do exactly that.

That made her wonder if the flirting had struck the same long neglected chord in him that it had in her…that sad, off-pitch *twang* of a sorely out-of-tune instrument.

Oh, yeah, she'd caught him looking at her mouth at the rodeo. Caught, too, how quickly he'd diverted his gaze, the slight flush in his cheeks after. And her girl bits—the ones she could still feel, anyway—had responded lickety-split, oh, yes, they had—

"He went off with your dad a few minutes ago, I have no idea why." And Dorelle had vanished the moment the short ceremony ended, probably chatting up anyone who'd stopped long enough to take a breath. Not for the first time it crossed Mallory's mind that her mother had never really been happy in LA, which had a nasty habit of swallowing people whole. And then spitting out the mangled remains.

"But it's okay, I'm good. No, I mean it," she said when Val frowned. A bit of a mama hen, that one. So Mallory smiled more brightly. "So go," she said, shooing them off. "Enjoy your wedding, for cripes' sake."

Val leaned over to give her another hug, then let Levi steer her back to the party, and Mallory's heart bubbled in her chest, a little, for the couple's happiness. It was obvious how truly in tune with each other they were. A real-life Hollywood happy ending, she thought, smiling. Nice.

And this was quite possibly her only chance to escape.

Fortunately, no one noticed. Because of the crowd and the fire merrily crackling in the hearth, all the outside doors were open, letting in sweet trickles of fresh, cool air. Having already noticed clots of attendees pooling in the courtyard and side patio, Mallory made her way back out front, to that wonderful veranda with its stunning mountain views. And indeed, the clear, autumn-scented air enveloped her like a hug, if a chilly one. She pulled closed her pashmina shawl—a birthday gift from Russell, many moons ago—then wheeled out toward the veranda's edge to take in the sun's lengthening rays drenching the massive front yard in that lush, peachy gold unique to New Mexico.

Smiling, she filled her lungs with air so clean, so bright, it sparkled, then released a long, slow breath, as close to peaceful as she'd felt in a very long time. Even if it was as fleeting as that great ball of fire rapidly sinking behind the mountains.

"You hiding, too?"

Twa-a-a-ang.

Chapter Eight

Most likely, if Zach had kept his mouth shut Mallory would've never known he was there. Except for one thing he'd started to feel a little creepy, watching her when she didn't know it. And for another…well, he supposed he at least owed her an apology. Because even though technically this wasn't a date, a gentleman doesn't abandon his guest.

Then again, a gentleman didn't entertain the kind of thoughts Zach was entertaining.

Because the moment she and her mother had arrived, every single thing he'd told himself the night before—all that stuff about logic and practicality and how what he had now was *enough*—had gone *ka-blam*. Not that he could've analyzed his feelings if you'd paid him. All he knew was, each time he saw her, smelled her, heard that laugh, his control slipped a little more, making him want to…

What?

To somehow absorb whatever it was that that had kept

her *her* despite everything that had happened. To be more like her. To be with her.

Alone.

And preferably naked.

Yeah. And hell, no.

And damned if his heart rate didn't kick up as she wheeled toward him, a slight smile on her lips. Not in any hurry, though—and he'd seen how fast she could go, so he knew the chair was no hindrance. The sun sliced across the yard, making her hair flame. The stark light wasn't particularly kind, but it was revealing. Honest.

Now it wasn't only his heart rate kicking up.

"If you recall," she said when she got closer, "I'm not real fond of crowds."

It took him a moment—because the blood flow wasn't exactly surging toward his brain—to remember what he'd said to provoke her response. Probably because he'd expected her to take him to task for ditching her.

"And yet you obviously like people."

The smile stretched. "I *love* people. Just not so many of them at once. In fact…"

Mallory moved closer before pivoting her chair to face the mountains. The temperature was already dropping with the sun; she rearranged that shawl, tugging it higher on her neck.

"Russell loved to throw these big parties. I much preferred intimate dinners, six people at the most. But more and more he kept coming up with some excuse or other for those dinners at the last minute, forcing me to cancel. Didn't take me long to realize he was doing it on purpose, that being in a small group forced him to actually relate to his guests. So much easier to mask who you really are in a crowd. And I really hate pretending."

"Isn't that a little weird, coming from an actor?"

She barked out a little laugh. "I do know the difference

between taking on a role and real life." Her gaze slid to his. "Where are the boys?"

"With Mom and Dad, last I saw. Although around here, everybody looks out for everybody's kids. Meaning nobody can get away with squat."

"A real-life example of 'it takes a village.'"

"Pretty much, yep." At her wistful expression, he asked, "Who's Landon more like? You or his dad?"

Her mouth pulled flat as she thought. "Hard to tell. Crowds don't really bother him, but he's good in one-on-one situations, too. I'm not sure he takes after either one of us, frankly. He's just...himself. Oh...wow..."

"What're you looking at?" Zach asked, twisting around to see what had caught her attention.

"This," she said, pushing herself a few feet down the veranda to a padded porch swing, its chains tinkling in the breeze. "We used to have one on our porch when I was a kid. I'd sit in it for hours, reading. Or just swinging and thinking." She sighed. "Had my first kiss in it, too."

Zach rose from the chair he'd been sitting—okay, brooding—in and came up behind her. "I'm guessing Dorelle doesn't know about that part."

"Don't kid yourself, that woman knows everything. Although I'm guessing she did *not* tell Daddy," she said, reaching for the chain, which only made the swing wobble even more. "Stevie Franklin. We were fourteen. And we both had braces. So, yeah. Awkward. Especially since the swing wouldn't stay still." She heaved a dramatic sigh. "It was two years before I kissed another boy."

"You're not serious."

"No, really, I thought it was disgusting and stupid." She chuckled. "Not to mention painful."

At that point, Zach expected her to roll away. When she didn't—

"I'm guessing it's been a while since you've been on one of these?"

"Not since I left Texas. Russell thought they were tacky."

"Screw Russell," Zach muttered, walking around her. "Can you transfer by yourself? Or do you need help?"

"I don't know, I've never tried. Obviously. Although I might be able to—" she wheeled closer "—if you could hold the stupid thing steady…"

Easier said than done. Because no matter how he held it, he couldn't make it stop wiggling. Which was only made worse when Mallory tried to grasp the arm or seat to make the transfer. A situation she seemed to find funnier the longer they tried to make it work. Finally Zach said, "This is ridiculous," and scooped her out of the wheelchair, and she linked her arms around his neck, laughing…and then he tried to lower them both onto the swing, only he lost his balance and they crashed into the cushion, the chains creaking with the stress.

She sucked in a breath. "Ohmigod, if this thing falls… I don't know, maybe you should get up?"

"Can't now, not with you on top of me."

"Oh, yeah?" Her grin spread warmth through his chest. Among other places.

"Yeah. Because some things can't be stopped once you start."

At that she lost it completely, howling with laughter. But at least the swing had stopped its violent quaking, even if Zach's heart had only gotten started. Especially when her eyes locked in his, her smile softening. He shifted, the idea being to set her beside him. Only she tightened her grip behind his neck.

"You know what I'd really like to do right now?"

"I can't wait to hear this," he said, and her eyes twinkled. Then she palmed his cheek, that simple touch immediately setting him on fire.

"It's also been a while since a boy *kissed* me on a porch swing."

"You don't know what you're asking, Mallory."

"Actually, I do… Oh." Her gaze darkened. "Sorry, I thought…" She huffed a sigh, then said, "And here's where I should probably get off your lap and pretend like this never happened. If, you know, I could actually do that—"

"Oh, God, no, honey—" Zach grabbed her hand and pressed it to his chest. "That did not come out the way I meant it. Because trust me, I've been thinking about kissing you, too. For some time, actually."

Her lips curved. "You don't say."

"God's truth," he said, and she chuckled, low in her throat. "But…it's been a while since I've kissed a girl, too. On a porch swing or anyplace else. And I—"

"Think far too much, is how you want to finish that sentence," she murmured, then curved her hands around his jaw and brought their mouths together.

And in that instant, he knew *kissing* her would never be enough.

This was definitely one of those moments, Mallory thought as the kiss instantly morphed from sweet to sensational, when you realize nothing will be the same. When your life switches from before to after, the demarcation as clear as between the river and the shore.

Oh, jeez, could the man kiss, she thought as his mouth moved so firmly, so sweetly under hers…his teeth gently grazing her lips as one hand tangled in her hair and the other splayed across her back in a move so deliciously possessive she could barely think straight. Barely breathe.

She reached for one of the chains, the cool metal soothing her heated palm. Kind of.

"I'd forgotten how well you country boys can kiss."

"I'd sort of forgotten myself," Zach muttered, and she grinned.

"Your glasses are all steamy."

He removed them, frowning at the fogged lenses for a moment before smiling up at her. A sad smile, though. Big surprise.

"Not what I expected when I came out here."

"Me, neither. But I'm a big believer in taking advantage of the moment."

One side of his mouth lifted. "So you go around kissing random men whenever the mood strikes?"

"Oh, Lord…not hardly." In fact, she'd shocked herself, coming on to him like she had. Taking that risk. Being the aggressor never had been her strong suit. And since the accident—

"What?" Zach whispered, stroking her hair away from her face. Clearly not caring that she was sitting on his lap. She wondered what was going on underneath her butt, since she couldn't feel much of anything down there. Didn't mean she couldn't feel other things, though, other places.

"There's only so much opportunity for lip-locking in a small town," she said. "Especially if you don't really get started until you're sixteen and you meet who you thought was the love of your life a year later." She sighed. "Meaning Russell was my first. And only. But like I said…" Her shoulders bumped. "Things had gone wonky between us even before…all this. Afterwards…" She shrugged again, then sighed. "And maybe you should get me off your lap before somebody comes out and sees us. Like your kids, maybe."

"Good point," he said, then maneuvered her onto the swing beside him, his arm resting on the back behind her neck. To her chagrin her feet didn't touch the floor.

"Jeez, I feel like I'm five years old again. And to think I used to be so proud of these legs."

"Bet you could benchpress a Ford pickup, though. The exercise equipment?" he said when she frowned.

"Ah. It's true, my upper body strength is off the charts."

Zach dug his boots into the floor in front of him, setting the swing into motion. A steady, easy motion, not the crazy jittering from before. "So you haven't...you know?"

His shyness was beyond cute. Especially considering that little necking session back there. "Six years and counting."

"Damn."

"You're telling me. What Russell never understood—or wanted to, more likely—was simply because things worked differently didn't mean they didn't work at all. Or that my brain shut down simply because a couple vertebrae got screwed up." To her annoyance, her eyes stung. "I'm the same person I was before, you know? Okay, so maybe I wasn't exactly hot to get it on those first few months, but afterwards... Dammit, sex is about more than body parts fitting together!"

Oops.

Zach put his glasses back on. All the better to give her a long, searching look, she supposed, before saying, "I know what you mean."

"So I take it you...?"

His fingers grazed the back of her neck, making her shiver. "First kiss in forever, remember?"

"Hey. I read. I keep up. So I gather kissing isn't necessarily a prerequisite to...other stuff."

"For some men, maybe. Not me. I happen to like kissing. A whole lot, actually."

"Somehow I got that."

Then his lips curved, slowly. And with great meaning. "In fact..." This time he took the lead, one hand cupping her cheek as he brought his mouth down on hers, and she opened to him immediately, brazenly asking.

And boy, did she receive. After what seemed like three hours, although in reality the sun hadn't even shifted all that much, they came up for air. Which she may have gulped for a little. What was it they said about when you lose one of your senses, the others become more acute? In her case, apparently the nerve endings in the still-working parts of her body had happily taken on the tasks of the parts that didn't. She didn't just tingle, she *burned*.

Praise be.

"Thanks."

Zach smiled. Looking a little less sad, maybe? For his sake, she sure hoped so. "For?"

"Not rejecting me," she said bluntly.

Frowning, he looked away for several seconds. But when he met her gaze again, anger darkened his eyes. "Okay, I realize however I say this, it'll probably come out wrong, so I'm just gonna take my chances. I've also gotta be honest about having issues with…whatever this is between us. But those issues have nothing to do with you. *Nothing*. Because what I see, when I look at you…is *you*. Just as you are. Inside and out. The chair…okay, it's part of who you are, but it's not you. And I sure as hell don't give a damn that you're in it. And…"

He scrubbed his free hand through his hair. "And the thing is…" A ragged breath pushed from his lungs. "You make me…"

Oh, dear Lord. "Hot?" Mallory ventured.

A faint smile touched his mouth. That incredible, beautiful mouth. "Like you wouldn't believe. But not because I've got some weird fetish," he added quickly, and she laughed. "What I'm trying to say, is that the chair isn't an obstacle. Neither is the reason you're in it. The obstacle is me. And you need to know that before…"

He seemed to catch himself. Mallory laid a hand on his knee.

"Before we do anything more?"

Another pause. "Do you want to?"

"You really have to ask?"

"Even knowing…?"

"*Especially* knowing," she said, and his puzzled gaze zinged to hers. She folded her hand around his fingers, smiling when he squeezed back. "For five years, people have twisted themselves inside out trying to figure out what they could do for me. Some people, anyway. Now here's an opportunity for me do the giving. No, listen to me, Zach," she said when he shook his head. "You got me back up on a horse. Gave me back part of myself I'd pretty much thought I'd never have again. So let me do this for you." She smiled. "But act now, because this offer isn't available to the general public, and only available for a limited time."

His throat worked for several moments before he said, "How?"

Her heart slammed up against her ribs, even as she somehow managed to calmly say, "Up to you. You're the one with the kids. And I'll be the other one with a kid in a few days. Narrow window, guy."

"You're really sure?"

"You know, my hands work just fine. And you're close enough for me to smack. Yes, idiot, I'm sure. But…are you?"

Zach looked away again, then heaved a sigh. "Not at all," he said, lifting her hand to kiss her knuckles. "And ninety percent of me is saying I'd be a fool to do this."

"And the other ten?"

That got another sigh, this one absolutely breaking her heart. "Thinks I'd be a fool not to." He palmed the back of his neck, shaking his head. "You have no idea, the war that's going on in my head right now. Between what I want and what's right. And until those two mesh in my head…" He lowered her gaze to hers. "I can't."

"Can't?"

"Okay, shouldn't." Another breath. "Won't."

"I understand." And oddly enough, she did. Of course, leave it to her to find the most honorable man on the entire planet in a town so small half the houses didn't even have real addresses. She gave him a little smile. "But at least I got a couple fabulous kisses out of the deal."

He chuckled. "Same here." Then he stood, holding out his hands. "Need help?"

"Unless I plan on sleeping out here tonight? Yep."

Once back in the chair, Mallory looked up into that strong, gentle face, finding herself wondering what it must've been like, being his wife. Being the focus of all that devotion. And for a moment she actually felt envious of a dead woman, God help her.

Except then she thought, if what she saw in front of her was the result of loving that hard, she wouldn't want to be the cause of that much pain for anything.

"You know, this is where I'd stand on tiptoe to give you a kiss on the cheek before making my graceful exit. But I can't exactly do that."

In the deepening twilight, she saw him smile before he bent over, close enough for her to inhale his scent. "How's this?"

She reached up to touch his cheek. "Still can't reach," she said, and he bent closer, his late-day whiskers scratching her lips, still sensitive from all that earlier kissing. Same as her heart, she thought, glad he couldn't see the tears brimming on her lower lashes. Not for herself, though. For him.

Which could only mean one thing—

"I'll go back first," she said, "so we don't start a gossip riot."

"Thanks," he whispered, standing straight again, and she could feel his eyes on her back as she wheeled away. As well as her heart swelling to the point where it felt like it might burst.

Yep, she was in love, all righty. In a way she'd never been before. In no small part because she'd never known a man like this before.

Well, poop.

After the wedding, the boys had wanted to play a little longer with Austin—because spending the last three hours together running around together hadn't been enough—and Zach was too mentally fried to come up with a reason why they couldn't. Val's former in-laws had taken the girls so Levi and Val could have a short honeymoon up in Durango across the Colorado border, his parents had left early, and frankly Zach didn't want to go home, either, to a house perfumed with too many memories, too many unrealized hopes and dreams. Normally he could hack it, but tonight…not really.

So here he was in their old childhood home, the three-bedroom cabin on the property that came with the foreman's job. Not huge, but adequate. Comfortable. Place hadn't changed much, though, since Zach and his brothers had lived there with their parents—same worn upholstered furniture, same even more worn rugs, same burn marks in the wooden floor fronting the stone fireplace from when *somebody* hadn't bothered replacing the grate and a red-hot log had tumbled out and nearly caught the carpet on fire. Not to mention that old Labrador retriever they'd had back then.

Said somebody came out of the kitchen with two mugs of coffee, handing one to Zach before—carefully—sinking into the middle sofa cushion with a huge sigh. The boys were all in Austin's room, lost in a world where a miniature toy car could take you anywhere you wanted to go, and a box of old Halloween costumes could change you into anybody you wanted to be. Too bad there weren't such things for grown-ups, Zach thought, morosely sipping his coffee.

His brother was close enough to prod Zach's foot with the toe of his own boot. "What's up with you?"

A question he'd never have asked when he would've only been five to Zach's twelve, thirteen to Zach's twenty. Funny how adulthood leveled things out. On that score, anyway. Although the brothers had grown closer since Levi's discharge from the Army that past May, the bond between the twins—and their feeling of comfort about sharing with each other—was much stronger than between Zach and them. At one time Zach and his other brother, Colin, only a year younger than him, had been best buds, but since he hadn't even heard from him in years...

Forcing a smile, he turned to the brother who *was* there and threw him a bone. "The wedding hit me harder than I thought it would. That's all."

Josh frowned. "You're not happy for them?"

"Of course I'm happy for them, that's not what I said. Jerk."

Josh shrugged. As he would. He never had been the type to take offense.

"Val's great. And great for Levi. But it's the first wedding I've gone to since..."

"Right," Josh said softly. "Sorry."

Of course, no way was Zach gonna talk about what'd transpired between him and Mallory. And not only because Zach hadn't completely processed it himself yet. Wasn't all that sure he ever would, truthfully. She'd never know what it took for him to turn down her offer. Then again, maybe she would. Only once before had he known someone able to burrow into his brain like that, figure out what he was thinking even before he did. It'd been scary as hell then, and it was a hundred times scarier now.

From Austin's room, he heard Jeremy taking charge of whatever game they were playing. The kid always played fair, though, never taking advantage of being the older one—

"So Mallory said her son's coming out next week?"

Zach was beginning to wonder if his skull was transparent. "Yeah," he said, taking a sip of his coffee and trying not to make a face. His brother couldn't make coffee worth crap. "Which reminds me—" he set the mug on the table in front of him, folding his hands between his knees "—she needs another horse. For herself, this time."

Because what'd happened between them didn't change that fact. Nor would Zach let it interfere with following through on what he'd started.

Josh grinned. "Kinda thought that was coming. She told me about you taking her out to Adrienne's place. She really needs an animal already trained for her needs, though. I can't help you there. I don't suppose Adrienne would sell one of hers?"

"Unfortunately, no. I already asked."

"Hmm…" His brother's forehead bunched for a moment, then he snapped his fingers. "Hold on—" He set his own mug on the end table, then leaned over to dig his cell phone out of his back pocket. "I seem to remember…" After several clicks, he turned the phone around to Zach. "You ever heard of this outfit?"

Squinting, Zach took the phone, shaking his head. Some horse farm down near Albuquerque. Josh stretched over the table to point at the screen. "That's what they do. Raise and train horses for special needs riders."

"Like what Adrienne does, you mean."

"Adrienne only trains horses for her own operation.

These folks train 'em to sell. Or donate, in certain cases. You should give 'em a call, see if they've got one that'd work for Mallory." He took his phone from Zach, crossing his arms high on his chest before sinking into the cushions again. Then a sly smile snaked across his face. "Might be a good excuse for the two of you to have a little time away together. Alone. I'm sure somebody will take the boys."

Heat stabbed at Zach's face. "What are you on about?"

"You know, next time you decide to make out with a girl you might want to pick someplace a little less public?"

Zach muttered a cussword that made Josh chuckle. "Who else saw?" he said, not daring to look at his brother.

"Nobody but me. I swear. I just happened to step outside for a second, and…" He shrugged. "And no, I'm not gonna blab, so you can wipe that 'I'm screwed' look off your face." A second passed before he said, "So what does this mean, exactly?"

Heaving to his feet, Zach swiped his jacket off the arm of the chair and shrugged into it. "Like you never kissed a gal just for the sake of kissing her."

The smirk faded from his brother's face. "Not talking about me, bro. Because you know as well as I do random encounters aren't your style."

"What I know is that I don't have to explain my actions to you or anybody else—"

"Very true." Josh stood as well, his fingers shoved in his jeans' front pockets, a frown gouging his forehead. "Long as they make sense to *you*, what other people think is of no consequence. But can I say one more thing?"

"No."

"From where I was standing it sure looked to me like you were having a damn good time. Maybe even having *fun*. And when's the last time you had some of that? Jeebus, Zach—it's not a crime to let yourself be happy again."

A dozen retorts playing through his head, Zach stared

his brother down for several moments before deciding the smartest choice was to keep his yap shut. "Thanks for the coffee," he muttered, then walked to the end of the hall to call his boys.

Because being *alone* suddenly sounded really appealing.

Except, as he went about getting his boys fed and bathed and in bed and read to—a process that seemed to take longer every night—he had to admit his brother's suggestion wasn't exactly *un*appealing. If impractical.

Not to mention illogical.

Really.

Then again, the woman still needed a horse…

Chapter Nine

"Hey," Landon said, squinting at Mallory on the laptop screen. "You look really nice. You going somewhere?"

Damn. He *would* call when she was on her way out the door, to go with Zach to a horse farm in Corrales, right outside Albuquerque. Just the two of them. Spending most of the day together. And, yeah, color her shocked when he'd made the suggestion, especially considering how their little interlude had ended. Then again, they *were* grown-ups.

Grown-ups with very grown-up yearnings that hadn't been met in a dog's age. Both of whom had very tender hearts right now, even if for very different reasons.

Could Landon hear her heart pounding? Lord, she hoped not.

Probably best not to tell him about Zach. Not yet. Now. Whatever.

Or, actually, the new horse, either. Hors*es*.

"Just out with a friend," she said, casually, praying she wasn't blushing. Some actress she was.

"Where?"

"Shopping." Two questions, two not-lies. So far, so good.

"What's her name? The friend?"

Crap. "*His* name. Zach. The guy you met on my phone?"

"For like a *second*." Her son's brow crinkled, almost the way he used to do when he was tiny, and for a moment she wished she could have that adorable, innocent toddler back. "Do you, y'know, like him?"

Mallory sputtered a laugh. "Of course I *like* him, he's my friend."

She could almost say that with a straight face, even. As long as she didn't think about the kissing. Or didn't think, period. So that was a *no*.

"Will *I* like him?"

Weird, how the kid assumed he'd meet Zach. Weirder, still, was how often Mallory had played out that very scenario in her head. Of course, twenty-four hours ago she would have called herself *muy loco* for entertaining such a thought.

"Well, I have no idea what his plans are while you're here," she hedged. "But I don't see why you wouldn't like him. He's a nice man. And he has two little boys of his own."

"Yeah? How old?"

Again, Mallory tried to keep her expression neutral. But it was no secret that Landon had always wanted siblings, even when he was tiny. "Seven and three."

"Oh," he said, sounding almost disappointed. She made a mental note to ask around, see if she could scare up some kids his age. Clearing her throat, she fiddled with the infinity scarf circling her neck. "So how's Dad?"

Landon shrugged. "Okay, I guess. He and Priscilla are going to drive up the PCH while I'm out there with you.

I heard him talking to her about some bed-and-breakfast up near San Francisco."

Her chest knotted. "Did he say which one?"

"Um…the something Valley Inn? Don't remember. Sounds like the most boring trip ever, if you ask me."

Well, color her flabbergasted. With a side order of pissed. Since the "something" Valley Inn—because, really, what were the odds that Russell would randomly pick another one with Valley as part of the name?—was the one he and Mallory had called "theirs," back in the day when they'd make that trip up the Pacific Coast Highway every couple of months or so, before Landon was born.

Where Landon had happened, actually.

"Mom? You okay? You look weird."

The doorbell rang, setting off Edgar and her mother's shushing Edgar as they both scurried to the front door.

"I'm fine. A little twinge, that's all."

"Mom. You can stop pretending, you know? I get it." His still smooth forehead crinkled. "I can *see* it. It's okay to say when it hurts."

Actually, more than one therapist—physical and psychological—had pointed out that not only could they not help her if she wasn't honest about her pain with them, but that being up-front with Landon would also help her son become more empathetic. Although clearly her sweet boy was that already, even without her help.

"Fine," she said. "I'll be sure to keep you in the loop."

"Good," he said, sounding like he was forty, for cripes' sake.

Of course, he had no idea the twinge this time had nothing to do with her compromised body. Although she could definitely feel it in the vicinity of her heart.

"Whatever," she said brightly. "And in any case, getting out will be good for me. Take my mind off…stuff. So I have to go, cutie-pie. But I'll call later, okay?"

"Okay." He grinned, his dimples twinkling. For the most part he looked like his father, but he definitely got her dimples. "Five more days! I can't wait!"

"Me, either, baby," she said softly, pressing her hand to her lips then her fingers to the screen. She doubted he'd let her do that much longer, but until she got the "Ewww, Mom!" reaction, she wasn't about to stop a moment before she had to. Right now, however, her baby only said "Bye!" and vanished from the screen.

In the reflection she saw Zach standing behind her, his hands in his pockets as usual, all steady and sturdy and studly, in his own quiet, bespectacled way. And annoyance with her ex tangled with that which she'd been feeling for this dude for some time, and for a moment she thought she'd combust. *Breathe, girl, breathe*, she thought, slowly spinning around. "Ready?" she asked.

And the look on his face made her stomach drop to her knees.

Or it would've, if she'd been standing.

Somehow or other, he'd forgotten how frickin' beautiful she was. Okay, not really, but seeing her now, her hair shining against the fuzzy blue scarf…his heart jammed somewhere in the vicinity of his throat. Just as a million words were jammed in his brain—what she'd said and he'd said and what his brother had said. Even what Heidi might've said, if her ghost or spirit or whatever could be here.

This was gonna be a lot harder than he'd thought.

"Zach?" Mallory said gently, her lips curved.

He actually gave his head a little shake. "You want to take your car or the truck? I'm good with either—"

"The truck's fine," she said, smiling, then wheeled past him toward the front door.

The surprise in her voice when he'd called had been

pretty obvious. Not that he blamed her. And he still wasn't sure about…any of it, really. What he was supposed to think, or do, or say, or even be. And he sure as hell had no idea what might happen. Or what he wanted to happen. But the more he thought about that conversation, the more he had to admit he'd turned her down far less out of nobility than from plain old stinkin' *fear*.

And that didn't sit well. At all.

The plan was, since the drive itself was over two hours, to check out the horses—there were two the owner thought would be suitable—have lunch and drive back. He noticed her purse was on the large side, but then, women often carried bags large enough to smuggle a pig in. Of course, what she didn't know was that he'd stuffed a few things in a plastic sack and tossed it behind his seat. You know, just in case.

And yes, that'd made him feel like a horny teenager hoping to score.

"So who has the kids? And Benny?" she asked once they were settled in the truck. Never mind that other, far more crucial questions shuddered between them. Or maybe not, maybe she was one of those women who, once rejected, simply moved on. Although according to his brothers, such women were rarer than white rhinos.

"My folks," Zach said. "Which they do a lot, anyway." He tossed her what he hoped was a not-nervous smile. "One reason why I'm kinda married to where I grew up."

"Family, you mean?"

He looked back out the windshield. He'd decided to take a series of back roads until they got past Santa Fe, since this far north I-25 meandered through the mountains like a drunk with no sense of direction. "Yeah."

"Makes sense. Especially with that family." She flashed a grin in his direction. "Not sure I'd want to leave a great support system like that, either."

"Of course, they've been on their best behavior around you, so…"

She laughed, then said, "And why else don't you want to leave?"

"Look around you."

Every second, it seemed, the panorama changed, a kaleidoscope of red rock outcroppings and blazing yellow and orange and gold leaves, of looming blue-green forests and luminous clouds clotted like sheep in the never-ending sky.

"It is pretty darned magnificent," she said. "Which is why I love it, too, you know."

"Still. It's not home for you."

She fiddled with her scarf for a moment. "Have you even been anywhere else?"

"Let's see…both coasts and pretty much everything in between. Canada. Mexico. Alaska."

He could feel her smile, almost literally warm on the side of his face. A smile that made him feel more relaxed and wound up at the same time. Figure that one out. "Texas?"

"Even Texas. Yes, ma'am, I'm better traveled than you might think. Mom and Dad took road tripping to new heights, determined we'd see as much of the country as possible. Then Heidi and I did our fair share, before the kids came. Always grateful to get back, though."

It took him a second to realize his voice hadn't caught when he'd mentioned Heidi. He wondered if Mallory'd noticed.

But at least the conversation got easier as they passed one tiny New Mexican village after another, through forests and mountains and the occasional field dotted with horses. They talked about their childhoods, their parents, the equal parts delight and terror of raising boys.

"Ohmigosh," she said, "one time, when Landon was

about three? He figured out how to unlock the front door and got outside. Mind you, I had trouble with that dumb lock, but it was no obstacle to ol' nimble fingers. Who'd dragged a chair from the dining room over to the door to reach the latch. Scared the stuffing out of me when I went to check on him in his room—since he was supposed to be napping—and he wasn't in his crib."

"Same thing happened to us with Jeremy. Only he was even younger. Maybe two? Still have no idea how he got out, but a neighbor brought him home. Nothing like opening your front door to find your child in someone else's arms."

"I believe the term you're looking for is heart-stopping. So how'd you prevent a repeat occurrence?"

"Installed more and higher locks. And basically didn't sleep for the next three years. Not that we had much before. You?"

"We installed these special security locks on all the exterior doors that practically required an advanced degree in mechanical engineering to get out of the house. Okay, so not really, but there was a time there when all I wanted was to be able to turn a doorknob and, you know, leave. Not to mention open a cupboard or a refrigerator without going through eighteen steps." She turned to him. "You ever wonder how babies ever actually made it to adulthood before all this stuff?"

"All the damn time. And I've still got one more little one to keep an eagle eye on. Although Liam isn't nearly as adventurous as Jeremy was. He gets into stuff, sure, but all in all he seems more content than Jeremy, who used to go looking for trouble like it was his God-given mission to find it."

She chuckled, then got quiet for some miles, her arms folded over her stomach. "You think you'd want more kids someday? If you remarried, I mean."

It wasn't an off-the-wall question, really. Or an unusual one, given the number of times other people had either insinuated it or outright asked. But given…things, it suddenly seemed much weightier than it might've been in other circumstances.

"Not that I'm real big on hypotheticals," he finally said, "but I suppose that would depend on a whole slew of variables. Number one on the list being the unlikelihood of me remarrying."

Zach could feel her gaze again. "You sound pretty definite about that."

"It's been more than two years. Nothing's happened to make me change my mind yet, so…" He shrugged. "In any case, Heidi and I had decided two was enough." He paused, then figured, well, hell, she'd asked him, so… "What about you?"

"Me? No. That is to say, I can't."

He glanced over. "Because of—"

"The injury?" She shook her head. "There were complications after Landon's birth." Her voice got soft. "Meaning no more babies for Mallory."

"I'm sorry."

"At the time, so was I. Although to be honest, even if I could have more kids… I'm not sure I would."

"Why not?"

She was quiet for a long time before she answered. "You know, it amazes me, how people are always saying how brave I must be. As if I had a choice in any of this. And maybe that's the way I present myself, I don't know. But not a day passes that I don't second-guess myself about how I'm doing with Landon. *What* I'm doing with him—"

"And that has *nothing* to do with you using a wheelchair."

Annoyance had propelled the words before he even

knew they were there. And he immediately realized how it sounded. Even before she gave him a look that made his ears hot. Then, sighing, she looked out the windshield again.

"Which would be my point," she said. "Don't get me wrong, I love my kid to pieces. But even before the accident I never felt as though I was giving him... I don't know. Enough? And that was with only one kid. Seriously, I do not know how people do it with a half dozen. Or more."

"Okay, for one thing? Any parent who tells you they've got this parenting thing nailed is lying through their teeth. We all make it up as we go along and hope for the best. And for another..."

He glanced over into wide, startled eyes, then back to the road, thinking how weird it was, the way she was so confident in some ways and not in others. Then again, he supposed he could say the same thing about himself. But they weren't talking about him right now.

"Watching you with Liam at the rodeo? Or more to the point..." To his surprise, his throat clogged. "Watching Liam with you? You've got nothing to worry about. In fact, I wish there was some way to play back that conversation I overheard between you and Landon the other day." His gaze briefly cut to hers again, then away. "The kid obviously adores you. So I think you need to scratch that one off your list of things to worry about."

She'd known this man for, what? Not even a month. And he'd already shown her more support than Russell had in nearly twenty years. Real support, that is. Not only what served his purpose. Something she hadn't entirely realized until this very moment.

Still. "Yeah, well, we butt heads like mad. All the time."

"Because he's *eleven*, Mallory. I was a pain in the ass

to my parents when I was that age. And the twins?" He wagged his head. "There were times I was surprised Dad let them live. Levi, especially. He and Dad had actual yelling matches."

"You're not serious."

"Nitro, meet glycerin. Mom was constantly coming between them."

Having watched the brothers horsing around with each other, the obvious affection they all had for each other... "I can't even imagine it."

"Trust me, I was there. And the thing was...at heart Levi was a good kid. A lot better than we even realized at the time. But finding yourself is harder for some of us than others. And some relationships need more time to ripen. That's all."

She smiled at him. "How'd you get to be so wise?"

He frowned slightly. "Not sure that's what I'd call it, but while everyone else was fighting? Or trying to break up fights? I was listening. Learning." He was quiet for a moment. "Decided I really wasn't a big fan of confrontation."

Mallory shifted in the seat, trying in vain to get more comfortable, since her upper back had been giving her five fits since Española. Then she smiled. "Make love, not war?" she said, smiling harder when his hands tightened around the steering wheel.

"Sure," he said, and she laughed.

And plunged, screw his distaste for confrontation. Although this was more about information-gathering, really. Or more to the point, her finding the courage to ask what this trip was really about.

"You know, I was pretty surprised when you called. Considering how we left things and all."

A brief smile flickered across his mouth. "I imagine so."

"So what made you change your mind?"

That he didn't ask about what—not to mention how long it took him to answer—told her they were probably very much on the same page.

"You're not the only one who needed to face a few fears," he said at last, and *bam*! The heat level rose at least twenty degrees in the truck's cab.

Willing her heart to settle down, already, Mallory looked at his profile. "And what fears might those be?"

A long pause preceded, "I wasn't going to say anything until we got where we're going. Maybe not even then, it all depended on, well, how things went, I suppose. Between us. But…okay. You know I really like you."

"Zach. We've already kissed and stuff. Moving on."

"Which part of me would very much like to do," he said, so quietly she nearly missed it. "Even if I'm not sure I really can. As I said."

"Fair warning, in other words."

"Yeah."

Mallory leaned forward, watching him. "But…?"

Another sigh. "I made reservations for lunch at this place near the horse farm." His hands worked around the wheel again. "At an inn."

She sat back, perversely enjoying his obvious discomfort. "As in, someplace with rooms? And beds?"

"Yep."

"And did you also book one of these rooms?"

"I…might have." Oh, dear. His cheeks were *so* red. "But it's just like when I took you to ride up at the Flying Star, no pressure."

She couldn't help her smile. "You're really bad at this, aren't you?"

"There's an understatement. Since I've never booked a room in the hopes of—"

"Getting lucky?"

"Being blessed," he said, very quietly.

Her eyes flooded. Also, she was so turned on she thought she'd explode out of her skin. Then her brow knotted. "Not even with Heidi?"

That got a very vigorous head shake. "Not before we were married, nope. And afterwards *she* always made the reservations."

"Aww..."

"Shut up," he said, a grin pulling at his mouth. Then Mallory sighed.

"There's one slight problem—"

"It's okay, I brought condoms."

"Good man. But no baby basket, remember? And I assume, given everything you've said..."

"It's been more than two years. So, yeah, I'm good." He turned to her, frowning. "So...?"

"There really is no delicate way to put this, but it's probably best if I don't eat...before."

"Oh. Right. Actually, I knew that."

"Really?"

"I, uh, did some research. Online. So I wouldn't look—or act—like a total moron."

"And that is the sweetest thing anyone's ever said to me. No, really." She turned away. "And it's a helluva lot more than my ex bothered to do. But I also think we should go see the horses later."

Confusion crumpled his brow. "Why?"

"Because now you've put this idea in my head, there's not exactly a whole lotta room for anything else."

His sigh practically enveloped her. "Me, neither," he said, and she felt tingles in places she hadn't felt such things in a very, very long time.

"Not a problem, sir. Since the room wasn't occupied last night, you absolutely can check in now if you'd like."

If the smiling woman drowning in Navajo silver-and-turquoise jewelry at the front desk wondered what was going on, Zach thought as he handed over his credit card, she was at least discreet enough not to let it show. Which is more than Zach could probably say for himself. Even though they probably weren't the first couple to use her fine establishment for a romantic assignation. For her, this was probably nothing to even bat an eye about.

For him, however…

"This place is gorgeous," Mallory whispered as they drove around through a forest of almost bare cottonwoods to their room, with its own entrance and a small, very private brick patio swathed in crinkly wisteria vines. God knew there were plenty of less fancy—and far cheaper—motels a half hour farther south in Albuquerque, but Zach would put out his right eye before staying in one of those places himself, let alone bring Mallory to it. He parked the truck, then went around to retrieve Mallory's wheelchair before lifting her into it, her scent alone enough to send his libido into overdrive. As if he needed any external provocation.

She wheeled onto the patio ahead of him, a little "Oh!" of delight falling from her lips as she took in the quaint, wrought-iron table and chairs surrounded by a dozen pots and halved whisky barrels overflowing with mums and pansies and other hardy, late-season plants. The air smelled of fireplace smoke and her perfume, with a slight overtone of whatever the barrels had once housed.

"Zach…" The word was a breath. Mallory lifted her face to his, her eyes shining. "This is so much more than I was expecting."

"Ex…pecting?"

She leaned forward to touch a huge purple pansy, quivering in the sunlight. "I might have a change of clothes in my purse."

He blinked. "And if we'd only looked at horses?"

Leaning back in the chair again, she seemed to think about this for a moment. "Not gonna lie, I would've been disappointed. For a little while, anyway. But you know, what you said before?" Her eyes met his. "About how there was no pressure? The same goes for you, too. At any point you feel you want to back out, I'm good with that. And if today's a onetime thing?" A breeze blew her hair across her cheek. She pushed it behind her ear. "I'm good with that, too."

Slowly, Zach closed the distance between them to squat in front of her, taking her hand in his. He pressed her knuckles to his mouth, his chest constricting at her soft smile. He knew she was sincere, that he could still back out and she really would be okay with it. Eventually, anyway. The problem was...he wouldn't be.

No matter which option he chose.

"Zach?" Amusement danced in her eyes.

"Hmm?"

She leaned forward close enough for her hair to brush his cheek. "Wheelchair sex can be fun and all," she whispered, "but you probably don't want your first time to be within hearing distance of the other guests."

And that, boys and girls, was all it took.

There was a lot to be said for patience heightening anticipation, Mallory thought sometime—okay, a lot—later. Because a chick in a wheelchair simply doesn't rip off her clothes and get down to it. For one thing, there were practical matters to tend to involving the bathroom and such, matters that would not be rushed, her frenzied hormones be damned. Then there was the internal debate about whether she should undress in the bathroom and wheel back naked, or let Zach do the honors, or what? Since they hadn't exactly discussed any of this. Criminy, it'd been nearly twenty years since her last first time. Back when her legs still worked—

"Mallory? Honey? You okay in there?"

She wondered which of them was more nervous, decided it didn't matter. She'd also reconciled herself to the distinct possibility that this would be a complete bust, for many reasons. But at least they could say they'd tried, right?

Still dressed, she opened the bathroom door, gulping at the sight of a shirtless, barefooted Zach. Ripped, no. Solid? Oh, hell, yeah. Scared? She was guessing yes. Then, his gaze locked in hers, he said, "What do you need me to do?" and she could practically feel the fear melt.

And so did she.

She wheeled over to the bed—since truth be told she had no more experience with wheelchair sex than Zach did—then transferred from her chair onto the mattress, her limp legs dangling off the edge. Heat surged in her cheeks; Zach knelt in front of her, palming her jaw. "What?"

"My legs aren't exactly pretty, Zach."

"It's okay, my brothers tell me mine aren't either."

"With that chest? How could they not be?"

With that, he stood and shucked off the jeans, revealing plaid boxers barely concealing a very hopeful bulge... and, yes, a pair of the palest legs she'd ever seen on a man. Too late, she clapped a hand over her mouth to stifle her laugh. Frowning slightly, Zach glanced down at his legs.

"There's a reason I never wear shorts."

"Except if you did," she said, giggling, "you might get some color on them. But at least yours *work*, for heaven's sake."

"There is that," he said, shrugging, and something powerfully sweet flooded her, that he could kid with her, be himself with her...that she could be *her*self with him.

Then he gestured toward her legs. "Okay, I showed you mine. Your turn."

"And if we want to do this before we're ninety you should probably help me."

"I can do that," he said, then crouched in front of her, unzipping first one boot, then the other, so slowly she thought she'd scream…and tossing first one, then the other over his shoulder where they thunked onto the patterned carpet covering a good chunk of the brick floor. Then he pushed himself up to cup her face and kiss her, and it was a celebration of tongues and spit and softness and heat the likes of which she'd never known. And would never forget. Especially when she caught the look in his eyes, the pupils dilated though they were, that told her he was still mightily conflicted about it all. Determined, but conflicted.

So before he changed his mind, she leaned back to unbutton her jeans—

"No, let me," he whispered, her stomach muscles flinching when his rough fingers slid across her skin. Then his mouth made contact with her belly button, which she shouldn't have felt but somehow did, someplace far beyond physical sensation…his kisses continuing south as he tugged off her jeans, then her panties, shifting her around so she was stretched out on the bed. She hiked herself up on her elbows, watching, tears cresting in her eyes as he stroked her thighs, her caves, worshipping their pitiful shrunkenness with his mouth, his hands. It should've been funny, this goofy guy wearing nothing but his boxers and glasses, making love to a pair of lifeless legs, but it wasn't. It was…

Amazing and beautiful and incredibly hot, and if she became any more aroused she'd combust.

"Hold on," she said, pushing herself into a sitting position, where she ditched her sweater and bra, the movement making things perk right up. Grinning, Zach sat back on his knees, adjusting his glasses, and by now her nipples were whimpering. "Well, that was certainly worth the wait." She threw a pillow at him. Which he caught and threw back. "So…in the Transmutant movies…?"

"No embellishment required, nope. Also…uh…" She glanced down, then back at him.

He took the hint. Laying her back against the pillows, he paid homage to her breasts in a way she'd only dreamed of for years, only more slowly, more thoroughly, more carefully than she *could* have dreamed…and every working nerve ending stirred from its long slumber, and…

No. Really?

Apparently so. Well, okay then.

Threading her fingers through Zach's hair, Mallory all but yanked him back to the breast he'd just left, pushing out, "Keep going…yes, oh, *yes*! Oh my heavenly *stars*…"

Of which she saw quite a few, yes, she did. And there was panting and gasping and a high-pitched screech that had her fervently hoping the walls were soundproof.

Afterwards, Zach cradled her in her arms. "Was that…?"

"It was."

"So you can."

She twisted her neck to look at him. His glasses were crooked. And smeared. "It's different for everybody. Some women can, some can't, some describe it as still a release, but different. All I know," she said, smiling, "is that I'm one very happy camper right now." Then she frowned. "Exactly how blind are you, anyway? Without your glasses?"

"You don't think it's kind of kinky?"

"I think I don't want to worry about them flying off or something. So you need to lose them. Also—" She reached over to snap the waistband of his boxers. "These."

"Done," he said, leaning over her to set the glasses on the nightstand, then shucking the drawers in a move much more smooth than she might've expected before wrapping her in his arms. And kissing her some more while she touched, teased, explored. Made him do some gasping of his own before he positioned himself over her.

"So what comes next?" he asked.

"You, hopefully. But you'll have to… Yeah, okay, I see you've got this," she said when he spread her legs. Which probably would've been like jelly, anyway, even if she hadn't been paralyzed. Then he was inside, and her eyes flew to his. "Holy hell. I can feel that."

He smiled. "Yeah?"

"Yeah. I don't know why, but I can."

His grin grew downright evil.

In the most perfect way possible.

As Mallory wrapped her arms around Zach and held him close, she shut her eyes, praying he'd find the same release in them she'd found in his.

In every meaning of the word.

Chapter Ten

By the time they'd gone out to the farm to see the horses—and for Mallory to buy the calmest chestnut mare in the world—they were both starving. So much so that for the first five minutes after their food came, they were too busy stuffing their faces to talk.

Which they were probably going to have to do eventually. If only to figure out what happened next. Or even if there was a *next*. For now, though, Zach was actually content to watch her devour her green chile chicken enchiladas as if she hadn't eaten in a year, chasing it with a chunk of sopapilla, drizzling honey inside the sweet, puffy pastry before popping it into her mouth.

Oh, *man*. That mouth…

There'd been a few—okay, more than a few—awkward moments, but also many that…weren't. Mind-blowing, was the term that came to mind. And a lot of laughter, as they tried to figure out what worked and what didn't. Why he'd thought she might be self-conscious, he had no idea. Instead she had no trouble urging him to try this or that or the other, even as she also, and repeatedly, asked what *she* could do, what *he* liked—

"What?" she mumbled as she chewed, her eyes bright. Even after an hour, she still glowed, a thought that made him ready to rumble all over again. Or still. He'd fully expected to feel guilty. Or at least something close to it. That he didn't...

He shook his head. "Nothing."

Mallory leaned closer, a drop of honey glistening at the corner of her mouth. "Like hell. I know what you're thinking."

"Oh, yeah?" Zach asked, taking a bite of his huevos rancheros.

A chuckle rumbled from her oh-so-magnificent chest before she said, "See, right here is where I'd play footsie with you under the table. If I could, you know, lift my foot. So imagine it. 'Cause I sure am."

The good news was, there were few other patrons this late in the day. The bad news was, there was little chatter to muffle their voices in the not-exactly-huge room. "You do realize," he whispered, "I now can't think of anything else?"

"That was the idea, bub," she said, and he smiled. Then, her attention drifting to a blue-black grackle searching for crumbs in the inn's courtyard, she sighed. "I didn't know..." Her cheeks pinking, she met his gaze again. "I never knew it could be like that," she said, her voice hushed. "Not in real life, anyway. And I don't only mean... now. I mean ever."

A frown bit into his forehead. "I didn't think I was doing anything special."

Mallory's gaze gentled. "You were paying attention to me. You...you gave a damn whether I was enjoying myself or not. The rest of it…that can be figured out. But not if only one person in the bed…" Her eyes watered. "*Cares.*"

Hell.

Zach reached for her hand, hating how loud his heart was pounding, hating the feeling that had nearly overwhelmed him back in the room, that he was losing control. Or, more likely, that he'd never had it. Mallory frowned at their linked hands, then withdrew hers again. "I'm sorry. This is so not how I pictured this conversation going—"

"But it did. So deal. And keep talking."

"You sure?"

"Mallory, for God's sake—"

"Okay, okay…got it." Then a soft, humorless laugh pushed from her mouth. "With Russell and me, I just kept thinking…shouldn't there be more?" Shaking her head, she poked at her enchiladas, then set the fork down to cross her arms, her brow furrowed when she looked across the table at him. "Then I started to wonder if there was something wrong with me."

Zach's fist clenched. "Your ex said that?"

"Oh, no. Never. He seemed perfectly okay with things."

"Did you tell him you weren't?"

"At first? No. Because I was young and inexperienced, so I figured it'd get better. Then as time went on and it didn't…" Her mouth twisted. "Whenever I brought up the subject, instead of trying to work it out, he'd withdraw." She smirked. "As it were. Until eventually, after Landon came… I think he felt once he'd given me a kid, he was done. To be truthful the accident didn't really change things on that score. Although it did give him an excuse."

Zach nailed her with his gaze. "Why didn't you ditch his sorry ass long before?"

"I guess…because I needed him? Thought I did, anyway. For a boatload of reasons that changed through the years. Took me a long time to realize how dependent on him I'd let myself get. And it actually wasn't terrible. Well, aside from the sex thing."

"That's kind of a biggie."

"True. But Russell opened doors for me I never, ever would have been able to open on my own, and I wasn't stupid enough to look that particular gift horse in the mouth. Besides, I was busy with my work, and then I had Landon, which gave me another, wonderful focus, and…"

She shrugged, looking so lost, so vulnerable, Zach's chest fisted…followed by another, even sharper cramp, that she felt comfortable enough with him to open up like this. He'd never felt more honored, and more frightened, in his life. Not even when he'd said "I do," not even when the kids were born.

Not even when her eyes had flown open in delighted surprise a moment before she fell apart in his arms.

Frowning, Zach crossed his arms high on his chest. "I can't help wondering why he married you to begin with."

"I fed his ego? He was in love with the idea of seeing his protégée succeed? You know, a Henry Higgins complex?" Her shoulders bumped again. "Who knows? I suppose we were more friends than lovers. No, that's not it, either—*colleagues*. And as I said, it wasn't awful. Until I was no longer who he'd married, I guess. Oh, and then I found out he was cheating on me."

"Damn."

"Yeah. Fun times."

"So the new wife…?"

"Not that new, as it turned out. To him, anyway."

Zach picked up his fork again to shove in the last bite on his plate. "Not that you're bitter or anything."

"I think *disappointed* is more accurate. Not easy for someone who…" Her eyes watered again. "Who doesn't accept defeat easily. Or failure."

"Which is why you won all those championships."

"Pretty much, yep. And when I realize something really is out of my control, that there's nothing I can do to make it right or change it…it kinda makes me crazy. What's so funny?" she asked, smiling.

He pointed to himself.

"Oh, yeah?"

"Like you wouldn't believe."

"Maybe we should start a club or something."

"Except we'd never be able to hold conventions because the planning committee would never be able to compromise on *anything*."

This time her laugh filled the room…and his heart. Except then she took a sip of her diet soda and said, very gently, "Can you tell me what happened? With Heidi?"

Zach was actually surprised it'd taken her this long to bring up the subject. He also supposed he owed her this much. What wasn't a surprise was that the timing didn't seem nearly as weird as he would've thought. Because this was Mallory, he supposed.

So he told her about how Heidi had decided to make a run into Taos to pick up some last-minute Christmas gifts, late at night after the boys were asleep. That she'd hit a patch of black ice and lost control of the car. How he'd refused to believe the sheriff, when he'd come to the house.

Tears glistened in Mallory's eyes. "Oh, Zach…" She reached for his hand, which he grabbed like a lifeline. "I can't imagine. And at Christmas…how on earth did you even get through it?"

"I'm not sure we did, truthfully. Holidays…they're still pretty rough. Because she loved them so much. Which seems so unfair for the kids. Especially for Jeremy."

"I'm sure," she said, then sighed. "How heartbreaking. For all of you. I'm so sorry."

He nodded, waiting out the stab, then lifted his eyes to hers. "What about you?"

"How I ended up like this, you mean?" He nodded, and her shoulders hitched. "Got too big for my britches, took on a slope I wasn't ready for. Missed a turn and…" Another shrug. "My ski didn't pop off like it was supposed to. Filed under 'crap happens.'"

Still holding her hand, Zach lifted it to his mouth, his heart twisting at her sad smile. He squeezed her hand, then let it go, nodding toward her plate. "You done?"

"Guess so," she breathed out, tucking her folded napkin underneath the rim. He waved for the check as Mallory checked the time. "So…if we leave now—" she lifted her eyes, luminous and hopeful and not quite as sad as they'd been a moment before, to his "—we'll be back by six?"

His logical side practically screamed, *Hell, yes, get while the getting's good.* His logical side knew the more he tried to make her happy, the more likely he was to break her heart. His *logical* side said what he was thinking was ultimately selfish, no matter how it might appear on the surface. That while he could give her this, he couldn't give what she most deserved. Especially after what she'd just told him about her marriage.

Except…

The check came; Zach tucked his credit card into the folder, handed it back to the waitress and said quietly, not looking at Mallory, "Room's ours until noon tomorrow, you know."

Her silence brought his gaze back to hers, the smile playing around her mouth instantly turning him inside out. Not to mention on. Except this was about more than that. This was about…sharing. Comfort. Kindness.

Living.

"And the boys? The dog? Your clinic?"

"Covered."

The smile stretched into a grin. "Meaning you had this planned all along."

"What can I say, loose ends drive me nuts."

Several beats passed before she reached across the table again. "So until noon tomorrow the real world doesn't exist. Deal?"

Zach could see in her eyes, hear in her voice, that she understood. That whatever this was, it was for now, this moment. And that she was good with that. A lot more than he was, he guessed. Then a smile tugged at his mouth. "Although…we just ate?"

Mallory pressed her napkin to her mouth to stifle her laugh, then lowered it and whispered, "Guess we'll just have to take our chances."

True, that, he thought, taking her hand to press a kiss in the center of her palm.

"It's nothing to worry about, Charley," Zach said to the bearded, middle-aged man on the other side of the exam table as the pitbull mutt slathered Zach's face with kisses. Dodging the hyperactive tongue, Zach bent his head to reinspect the scrape along the dog's side where he'd side-swiped a branch. "The wound's already healing, in fact."

"But he keeps licking it so much…"

"It's what dogs do," Zach said kindly, scratching the grinning beast's neck underneath his blue bandanna. And if the poor guy's synapses were firing more regularly, he'd know this, since the Iraq War vet had always had dogs. "But I could give you some antiseptic ointment to put on it, if you like."

Charley blinked. "How much would that set me back?"

"You know, I've probably got some free samples around somewhere. But honestly? I'm not sure it'd do much good. And then Loco'd have to wear a cone so he wouldn't lick it off. And you'd hate that, wouldn't you, boy?"

His butt wagging, the dog woofed and gave Zach another slurp. "Tell you what—" Zach heaved the stocky dog off the table, then straightened. "If you notice any change, give me a call. You've got my cell number, right?"

"I think so…"

Although he'd given the guy at least ten cards before, Zach pinched another one from the holder on the counter and handed it over. "Anytime, Charley. I mean it."

"Okay." He looked down at his panting dog, his forehead crunched. "But you're sure…?"

"As sure as I can be."

Relief flooded the man's dark eyes. "So how much I owe you?"

"What'd we agree on last time? Five dollars, wasn't it? Go on and settle up with Shantelle, and call if you need anything."

"I'll do that, Doc. And thanks."

As Charley shuffled out, Zach released a sigh that had nothing to do with the man or his dog and everything to do with that trip to Corrales with Mallory the other day. As in, he could barely think of anything—or anyone—else. Why in God's name had he thought giving in to his need would somehow alleviate it, release the pressure, instead of intensifying it?

Bringing his loneliness into even sharper focus.

And Mallory's being so damned understanding only made everything worse—

Levi knocked on the door, a leash wrapped three times around his other hand, at the end of which a coonhound mix was clearly torn between wanting some lovin' and wanting to run for the hills.

Zach could relate.

"Come on in," he said wearily, and his brother frowned. Again, the seven years' age difference meant squat when the "little" brother had served three tours in Afghanistan. Also, in contrast to the cupid-like curls framing a sharply planed face, Levi was the biggest and broadest—not to mention the baddest—of the four of them.

His brother tugged the dog into the exam room, where the beast promptly stood on his hind legs to give Zach a hug, a move the dog would undoubtedly soon regret.

Levi speared Zach with a don't-even-try-to-pull-one-over-on-me look. "What's going on?"

"Nothing," Zach said, ignoring the look as he readied the dog's rabies shot. "How was the honeymoon?"

"Too damn short." Levi crossed his arms. "Mom says she and Dad had the boys for the night while you took Mallory down to Corrales to buy another horse?"

"They did."

"Dude. Corrales is less than three hours away."

Zach held up the syringe. "And I could stab you as easily as the dog, you know. Get Radar up on the table, then help me hold him."

After the beast had been duly poked—and had duly peed on the table—Levi sat on the bench seat across the room comforting the dog, now lying across Levi's lap and regaling Zach with reproachful eyes.

"Guilt's a bitch, isn't it?" Levi said softly.

His face warming, Zach tossed pee-soaked paper towels into the medical waste bin, then washed his hands at the sink. "Where do you come up with this stuff?"

"Mom. She said you wouldn't even look her in the eye when you picked up the boys. Never mind that since a) you were gone all night and b) she knew you were with Mallory, it's not like this is some big secret. Although *big* is exactly what it is. For you, especially."

"You've got some balls, you know that?"

"Yeah. I do. Because I've been there, remember? And no, I'm not talking about staying out all night with a girl. Woman. Even if you weren't thirty-four, for cripes' sake."

Zach grabbed more towels to wipe his hands. "Not that this is any of your concern. Or Mom's."

"Have you met our family? And in any case, I know from guilt, bro. Falling for your best friend's wife?" His head wagged.

"Val was widowed, Leev—"

"And so are you. Doesn't mean you don't feel like you cheated on Heidi."

"That Mom's theory?" Zach said drily. "Or yours?"

"A mutual conclusion."

Zach glared. Then sighed. "For God's sake, it was just...a thing."

"Was? Or is?"

The edge of the exam table biting into his palms as he leaned on it, Zach met his brother's gaze. "God knows I'm no relationship guru, but nothing spells disaster like two baggage-laden people trying to make something work between them. Not to mention we're not a couple of kids with no ties, no obligations—"

"At least you admit to the baggage."

"Kinda hard to ignore." Zach straightened, stuffing his hands in his lab coat's pockets. "So don't go reading more into this than there is. Or could be. Because that ain't happening."

After a moment, his brother shrugged, then shoved the dog off his lap and stood. "If you say so."

"Dammit, Levi—"

"So you still seeing her? Or was that little trip to Corrales a one-and-done?"

"And what part of *none of your concern* are you not getting?"

"Oh, I'm getting plenty. As are you, I'm gathering. And man, I wish you could see your face right now. But there's one piece that doesn't fit."

Zach sighed. "And what's that?"

Grabbing the end of Radar's leash, Levi walked over and clapped his hand on Zach's shoulder. "You don't have 'things' with women, Zach. Me, sure. Well, used to. Josh, absolutely. But you?" He shook his head. "Not your style. So you can put any slant you want on whatever you've got going with Mallory. Doesn't make it true. And if you can't be honest with anyone else, at least be honest with yourself."

Levi was almost out the door before Zach said, "It's not that easy."

His brother turned back, giving Zach a look that was almost pitying. "From what I could tell you were spoiled, with Heidi. With how effortless things were between you. So now maybe you're being asked to step up your game, and it scares the bejezus out of you. I get that. But guess what? It won't kill you. And from what I've observed about Mallory? She's more than worth the effort. And speaking of balls—no point in having 'em if you don't use 'em."

His brother hadn't been gone five seconds when Zach's phone buzzed. And at Mallory's soft, "Hey, there," his throat clogged with a tangle of emotions he couldn't even begin to sort out.

"Hey," he said back, hoping he sounded normal. Because he immediately realized his brother was right, that "casual" went against everything Zach believed in. Which meant—

"You busy?" she said.

"Nope, between appointments. What's up?"

"Well, um… Landon came in a couple days early—"

"Really? That's terrific."

"I know, right? But…" Then he heard it, a hesitation in her voice that shouldn't be there. Not after everything they'd done with each other. For each other. Guilt stabbed, but from an entirely different source. "But I was wondering if you'd like to bring the boys over for dinner tomorrow night? If you'd be okay with that, I mean."

Her offering him space should have felt far more reassuring than it did. "Why wouldn't I be?"

"Because…the last thing I'd want is for you to feel you're being manipulated into something you're not comfortable with."

Pushing out a sigh, Zach lifted his glasses to massage the bridge of his nose. "That's not possible," he said softly. "And I'd love to meet Landon in person. So would the boys, I'm sure. But just out of curiosity—what've you told him?"

"That we're friends. Which is true. Right?"

Irritation pricked behind his eyes, that his goal—to bolster her confidence, help her overcome whatever was keeping her from reclaiming her full self—had somehow backfired. Sure, he heard the humor behind the question, but he wasn't a total moron, he knew a defense mechanism when he heard it. Or rather, recognized it.

And he had no earthly idea how to fix this mess of his own misguided making.

"Always," he said. Even if in their case "always" came with an inevitable end date. "What time do you want us there?"

"Six or so is fine. So see you then?"

"You got it."

Zach disconnected the call, frowning at his phone for several seconds.

Why on earth had he thought making love to her would set him *free*?

"Who was that?"

Glancing up at Landon, who'd come up beside her in the living room, Mallory grabbed a fistful of his long-sleeve T-shirt to tug him closer, wrapping one arm around his waist.

"Zach. I invited him and his boys to dinner tomorrow night."

"Oh. Okay. C'n we go see the horses again?"

Guess it was no secret where his priorities lay. As witnessed by his delighted "No, way!" when he'd first seen them. "We were just down there, goof."

He gave her that adorable grin that'd been slaying her since he was six weeks old. As it undoubtedly would untold numbers of females in his future, God help her. And him. "Please?"

In reality, he could go see them himself—he was eleven, after all. A big boy. And the pasture wasn't far. But from the moment she and Dorelle picked him up at the Albuquerque airport, it'd really hit her how much she'd missed him. Meaning she didn't want to spend a single moment apart she didn't have to.

"Okay. But go put on more clothes, it's chillier here than you're used to."

Another grin. "I noticed."

Edgar prancing at his heels—the dog clearly hadn't wanted to leave his boy, either—Landon returned in an LA basketball hoodie that six months earlier been too big. Now bony wrists protruded from stumpy sleeves, the bottom barely skimming his jeans' waistband.

"You seriously need to stop growing," Mallory said, and he giggled. Although was it her imagination, or was that giggle deeper than she remembered? As though he'd aged ten years in six weeks.

Or she had.

"It smells so good here," Landon said when they got outside, where the mingled scents of damp earth and decaying leaves embraced them like best friends. Spinning

around on one foot, he sucked in a deep breath. "Like…
like the earth is supposed to smell."

"Now you know why I love it."

"Yeah."

Bundled up in a lightweight down vest over her hoodie,
Mallory wheeled down the ramp off the deck onto the path
she and Zach had wandered along that first time he'd come
out to check on the stables. Without too much trouble she
could see him sitting at the base of that apple tree, his
expression one of calm acceptance as she told him about
Landon, why she'd decided it was best that he stay in LA.

Of course, since the man was camped out in her thoughts
24/7, anyway…

There was a time when she'd been optimistic to the
point of stupid, believing if you simply wanted something
enough, it'd work out. Age and experience had made her
much more pragmatic, however. She knew Zach's grief
was far too deeply embedded for her—or anyone else—
to simply wish it away. Still, she'd do anything to ease the
darkness inside him. Permanently, that is—

Occasionally kicking at a stone in the path, Landon
chattered away about school and his friends and his life
as they made their way to the small pasture where the two
horses grazed. She smiled as she listened, grateful that he
sounded like a normal, happy sixth grader, clearly much
less stressed than before. Not that he'd said anything, then
or now, about the toll the situation had taken on him. He
never had been a complainer, bless his sweet soul. Like
her, she thought. But a mother knew these things. Relief
flooded her, that she'd made the right choice. For now,
anyway.

"So they don't live in the stables?" he said, approaching
the fence. Both horses flicked their ears before deciding
to amble on over, check out the new human. Clearly in

love, Landon giggled when first one, then the other horse nuzzled his head, warming Mallory's heart.

"Only at night. Because how would you feel, having to stay in your room all the time?"

"Good point. So they just eat the grass and stuff?"

She wheeled up to the fence, handing him a piece of carrot before holding another one out to Macy, the calm, precious four-year-old mare whose previous owner had moved into a facility where she couldn't take him.

"Mostly, yes. At least in the warmer months. This growth is too old and neglected, though. So I'll have to supplement until spring, when the land can be tilled and replanted."

His eyes swung to hers. "That mean you're gonna stay here?"

Landon's words knifed straight through her, as she realized exactly how attached she'd become to the little farm, the plans she'd made without even thinking of the ramifications—that somehow she'd gone from thinking in terms of vacation home to *home*, period.

And that was the sound of her heart being slowly ripped in two.

Smiling, Mallory told him the truth. As much as she could, anyway. "I really like it here. I always have. I guess it reminds me of my childhood, a little. However..." She angled the chair to face him. "I miss you. Constantly. So I'm still trying to figure out how to make this all work out." He let her take his hand when she reached for it. "You seem a lot less fried."

Landon let go to climb up on the fence next to his horse. "Maybe. Although this new school?" The private school Russell had paid a pretty penny for Landon to attend. "The classes are whipping my *butt*. But the kids are cool, so..." He shrugged.

"And the teachers?"

"Hard. Like I said. But fair. And what's that you always say, about challenges making us stronger? So it's all good. Anyway—when can I ride him?"

"It's too late today. But tomorrow for sure."

"Cool. And you're gonna ride with me?"

"That's the plan. Although you and Grandma are gonna have to put the ramp together."

He scoffed. "Grandma?"

"Hey. Don't you be dissing your grandmother. This is the woman who built me a clubhouse when I was ten—with no instructions—from some scrap lumber we had lying around."

"Really?"

"Yep. Grandma is fierce. She's hardly gonna be intimidated by a little old ramp that's basically like a big Lego set. So the two of you have got this, baby."

Landon giggled again, then tromped over to plop in her lap, as he'd been doing from the moment she'd reassured him he couldn't hurt her. And he still couldn't, despite between roughly three times bigger than he was at six. That he still wanted to, however...

He looked around, then released a contented sigh. "I'm glad I'm here."

"You and me both, kiddo."

Chapter Eleven

Seated at the big wooden dining table across from this Zach person, Landon was kind of having a hard time focusing on his fried chicken, even though he hadn't had fried chicken in forever since Priscilla was all "Ew, *fried* food?" Also, he was starved from the high mountain air and riding Waffles and stuff. But between feeling weird that he hadn't told Mom about everything at home and this so-called "friend" of hers...

Seriously, did Mom really think he wouldn't pick up on whatever was going on between her and Zach? It was like when Dad had acted all nervous and stuff when he'd told him he and Priscilla were getting married. Like Landon hadn't seen *that* coming from ten miles away. Although he wondered if Mom had. If she'd even known how long Dad had been seeing Priscilla. Of course, Landon wasn't supposed to have known, either. But he wasn't stupid, you know?

Not that Zach and Mom were acting all lovey-dovey or

anything. But Landon could tell. By the way Zach smiled at Mom, sitting at the head of the table—it was just easier, with her chair and everything—by the way Mom's eyes got all funny when she looked at him. By the way they laughed, like they shared some secret joke. And he hadn't heard her laugh that much since...well, he couldn't remember when.

Also, he'd sure never seen her look at Dad like that. Of course, Dad was a jerk, but still. And, yeah, Zach had helped Landon ride Waffles earlier, and he'd been real nice and patient and stuff. But Landon didn't know anything about this dude, and that made him feel all jumbled up inside—

Oops. Busted. Landon ducked his head, but not before Zach obviously noticed him staring at him. Shoot, now his face was all hot. He caught Zach's smile, though. A nice smile. Real. Not like the ones grown-ups gave kids when they wanted to pretend they were friends with you because, say, they liked your dad.

"So you guys have any plans for the week?"

Zach had directed the question to him, not his mom. And again, like he was really interested, not like he was trying to suck up.

Landon glanced at Mom, who actually looked kind of relaxed. "Um...you said some of the Indian pueblos, maybe?"

"I did. And to Santa Fe, of course." She turned to Zach. "You and the boys want to tag along?"

He shook his head. "I've got either clinic hours or ranch visits for the next several days. And Jeremy has school." Seated beside his father, the older boy made a face for Landon's benefit. "And historic sites are kinda lost on a three-year-old."

"Another time, then," Mom said, smiling at Jeremy. Then she took a bite of potato salad and said quietly, "I also thought we might go up to the resort," and Zach gave her a weird look.

"The resort?" Landon asked.

Mom cleared her throat, then pressed her napkin to her mouth. "The ski resort. Where I had my accident. It's absolutely beautiful up there—the views are incredible. It's where…it's where I first fell in love with the area. Why I wanted to buy a vacation home here."

O-kay… Landon got the definite feeling there was more to what she was saying than what she'd said. Especially given the expression on Zach's face. What the heck? But all Landon said was, "Awesome," as Zach's littlest boy, in a booster seat beside Landon, started giggling like crazy at something Grandma had said or done. The kids were both pretty cute, Landon had to admit. Of course, generally speaking he liked little kids. Unless they were brats, then not so much. Mom had told him about their mother—that must've been so hard. Although he guessed the little guy—who'd slid down from his seat to go to his dad—probably didn't remember her.

Draped across Zach's legs, Liam disappeared except for his red curls. Then he started playing peekaboo with Landon, popping up and giggling, then vanishing, then popping up again. Landon couldn't help but laugh.

Zach gave Landon one of those smiles again, then lugged the little boy onto his lap. "What're you doing, goof?" he said, grinning, then making eat-you-up noises in the little guy's neck.

"Daddy!" he said over the giggles. "That tickles! Do it again!"

So he did, over and over. Like there was nothing he'd rather do than play with his kid.

Suddenly feeling like he was suffocating, Landon asked to be excused, then went outside to sit on the deck steps. Edgar followed, plastering himself beside Landon's hip

with a huge doggy sigh. It was frickin' freezing, and practically pitch-dark, but he didn't care. He pulled Edgar into
his lap, his chest pinching at how much he missed his three
mutts back in LA with a dog-sitter.

Then he heard footsteps behind him. Great.

"Your mom said you'd probably want this," Jeremy
said, handing him the throw from the sofa.

"Thanks," Landon muttered, not wanting to be rude.
And anyway, the blanket felt good as he wrapped up inside it with the dog.

Sucking on a Popsicle, Jeremy plopped onto the step
beside him, offering Landon a second one.

"A little cold for these, doncha think?"

The younger boy shrugged. "I'll eat it if you don't want
it."

"No, that's okay." He took the Popsicle and started
slowly peeling off the wrapper. "Thanks."

"You're welcome. How old are you?"

"Eleven. Twelve in January. You?"

"Almost eight. My brother's three."

Wadding up the wrapper to stick in his pocket, Landon
smiled. "Cute kid."

"Yeah, I guess. Except when he has meltdowns. Those
are *not* pretty."

Despite feeling all knotted up inside, Landon laughed.
Frankly, he was dying to pump the kid for more information about their parents, but he seemed a little young for
that. If he even knew anything—

"So do you like my dad?" he said. "Because I think
your mom likes him a lot."

What the heck? Landon glanced over at Jeremy, slowly
swirling the multicolored Popsicle in his mouth.

"Why? Did somebody say something?"

"N'uh-uh," the kid said, shaking his head. Edgar stuck
his head out of the blanket, sniffing the air. Because food.

Jeremy reached over to scratch him behind his ears, getting slobbery fingers for his efforts. "But I can tell. Can't you?"

"Yeah," Landon said, chomping off the top third of the Popsicle, the sharp cold giving him an instant brain freeze. "And I have no idea about your dad, I just met him." Then, because he didn't want to sound mean or anything, he added, "He seems pretty nice, though."

Jeremy nodded, then held his treat in front of him, twirling it so it sparkled in the landscape lights out in the yard. The dog crawled off Landon's lap, hopeful. Jeremy let him have a lick, so it was all cool. "So's your mom," the boy said, pulling back the Popsicle before the dog ate the whole thing. Then he licked right where Edgar had. "And grandma. She's really funny."

Landon felt his mouth pull up in a smile as the dog crawled back into his lap with a little groan. "I guess she is."

"Anyway…" Jeremy gulped the last bite, swiped his hoodie sleeve across his mouth, then looked around behind him, as if to make sure they were alone. "A couple days ago," he said, hugging his knees, "Liam and me stayed with our Gran and Gramps while your mom and my dad went to get your mom's horse? And I heard them talking after I was supposed to be asleep? About how they wished it'd work out between your mom and my dad, on account of him being all alone after my mom died."

Landon waited until his brain stopped buzzing before he said, "Doesn't that freak you out?"

Jeremy seemed to think about this for a minute, then slowly shook his head. "I guess it would feel weird and stuff, having another mom. But… I don't know. I think it'd be good, too. Mostly." Then he sighed and repeated, "I don't know."

For some reason that got Landon's hackles up. "My

mom's not staying here, you know. This is only a vacation home." At least, that's what she kept saying. What he'd always assumed. But seeing the way she looked at Zach…

His stomach got all twisted up. What if something really was going on between them, and she didn't want to come back to LA? Yeah, okay, in some ways things were a lot calmer when she wasn't around, but the downside was, she wasn't around. So he'd already planned to convince her she needed to come home. Even if he hadn't entirely decided how much to tell her. But he couldn't imagine living here—

"There you are," Zach said behind them, and Jeremy got to his feet. So did Landon, although between the dog and the blanket, he kind of got tangled up and nearly fell over. Zach grabbed him, his hands real steady around his arms. "You okay?"

"Yeah. Sure."

Zach frowned at him, then said to Jeremy, "Why don't you go on into the kitchen, see what all Dorelle's got for you guys to take home. I'll be there in a sec and then we'll head out."

After Jeremy left, Zach pushed back his jeans jacket to stuff his hands in his front pockets. Somehow he managed to look kind of nerdy and cool at the same time, with his glasses and everything. "And I repeat," he said in his low, soft voice, "are you okay?"

Landon half wanted to grill the man, find out if what Jeremy had said was true. Except little kids weren't exactly reliable sources. And the last thing Landon wanted was to sound totally whack. Even if Jeremy had only been saying what Landon was already thinking.

So he decided to play it cool. For now, anyway. Grownups were gonna do whatever they wanted, anyway, right? Except he couldn't remember the last time his own father had asked if he was okay. Like he really meant it, anyway.

"You probably need to get back to your kids."

"They'll be fine for a few minutes." He smiled. "I usually have to pry them away from your grandmother, anyway."

"So they've been here before?"

"It's a small town. Every time you turn around, you run into half of it. And I think my boys filled a gap until your grandmother had you to spoil again." He shifted his weight, standing more firmly on both feet. "You did real good on Waffles earlier. I can already tell, you'll make a great rider someday."

For some reason, the praise made Landon feel warm all over. "Thanks. I've always liked horses, even though I wasn't around them much."

"That's because you're your mama's son."

"Yeah, she showed me her prizes and stuff. I guess she was pretty good."

"That would be my take on it."

"She also said you're the one who got her to ride again."

That got another smile. "All I did was set things in motion. Your mother did the rest. Because if a woman doesn't want to do something, no way on God's green earth is a man gonna convince her to do it."

There went that warm feeling again, partly because Zach wasn't talking to him like he was a little kid, partly because what he said about women—or at least, the ones Landon knew—was so true. From what he could tell, Zach was pretty cool. That didn't mean, however, Landon wanted another stepparent. And it was gonna drive him nuts until he knew for sure what was going on.

Except he sure wasn't gonna find out now, not with Zach's kids waiting for him. Although...

"You suppose I could go with you sometime while I'm here? When you go out to ranches and stuff?"

Zach looked at him for several seconds before he said, "Just you and me?"

"Yeah. I want… I'm thinking I might like to be a vet, maybe. So I'd like to see what one does."

He smiled. Kind of. "Okay, then. I'll check with your mom and we'll coordinate schedules."

"Really?"

The smile got a little bigger. "Yes, really." Zach briefly squeezed Landon's shoulder and walked back inside, leaving Landon feeling…well, kind of good, actually.

Even if more confused than ever.

Mallory followed Zach out to his truck, sitting with her arms folded across her middle as he got Liam buckled in while he waited on Jeremy, who'd said he needed to pee. Once he had the toddler settled, he turned back, his breath puffing around his face as he frowned down at her.

"Your boy tell you he asked to go with me on one of my runs?"

"Ah. I wondered what that little confab on the deck was about."

Zach smiled. A tired smile, she thought. "Yeah, he said he was thinking about becoming a vet."

"Heh. Last week he wanted to be an architect. But then, he is eleven."

"What he is, is all balled up about tonight. Why I'm here." Zach's voice softened. "What's going on between us."

Just the words "between us" made those nerve endings still in touch with her brain jump to attention. But she wasn't about to read more into it than there was. Or could be. "So…?"

"I'm guessing I'm about to get grilled. You okay with that?"

"Him grilling you?"

That got a brief laugh. "No, taking him with me. Maybe watching me stick my hand up some mare's butt."

"You kidding? You'll make his day."

He chuckled. "So what's your schedule like?"

"The ruins've been there for centuries, they'll wait a day or two."

"Tomorrow morning, then? I'll pick him up after I drop Jeremy off at school?"

"Sounds good." Figuring it was safe, in the dark, Mallory reached for Zach's hand, wishing she could kiss it. Kiss him. Do a lot more than that. "So what're you going to tell him?"

Smiling, he entwined their fingers. "Haven't figured that part out yet."

Not that she'd expected some sort of declaration, but still. She sucked in a breath and said, "A warning, though. My mother's intuition tells me he's putting on an act for my benefit."

Frowning, Zach let go to stuff his hands in his back pockets. "What kind of an act?"

"I'm not sure. Although…it's almost as if he's being *too* sweet. Too…agreeable. Not a single head-butt since he's been here." A breath left her lungs. "As I said, it's only a hunch. I know what he says, that everything's fine, but…"

"You don't believe him."

"No."

"And you want me to pry?"

"And is it weird, that you don't sound even remotely bothered by the idea?"

"Heh. My mother used to *pay* me to dig up dirt on my brothers. You are looking at the master, lady."

Mallory laughed. "I'll bet. But, no. Because that *would* be weird. Figured you could use a heads-up, however."

He nodded, then checked the door, as though wondering where his son was, before leaning against the truck's bumper. "So you're taking Landon up to the resort?"

A smile pulled at her mouth, even as her heart punched into her throat. "Can't put it off any longer. Especially since that's part of the reason I took a house here. I need closure, and I think he needs..." She paused. "Context, maybe? Or that could just be crazy talk."

"Doesn't sound crazy at all. Not to me."

"No, I guess it wouldn't. Considering it's you I have to thank for shoving me off my butt to begin with. Metaphorically speaking, anyway. Who got me up on that horse. Who made me realize I had a lot more fears to handle than I wanted to own up to. Who..." Mallory's eyes stung. Hell. Leave it to her to turn a simple goodbye into some reality show emotion fest. "Who's been the first person since my injury to see past it."

Oh, dear Lord...the look on his face... Finally he said, "I don't believe that. Your mother—"

"Has been a rock, absolutely. And I'm more grateful for her support than I can say. But you're more like..." She smiled. "The river that rushes around the rocks, sweeping along everything it its path. And apparently that's exactly what I needed. Not only to be accepted as I am, but to be pushed past that. So thank you."

"I..." Zach pushed out a nervous laugh. "I don't know what to say. Other than—"

"You weren't doing anything special?" she said, teasing. "No, you were simply being who you are. Which for this woman is pretty darn special."

In the deep silence of an autumn country night, Mallory could hear the hiss of inhalation, the almost whistled exhale as Zach shook his head. Then he walked back to her, squatting in front of her to take her hands in his, and in the dull glow of the porch light she could see the apology in his eyes.

"You're pretty darn special, too, honey," he whispered, gently kissing her fingers before levering himself to his feet again, not five seconds before Jeremy finally appeared, hitching up his pants as he tromped out to the truck. Zach opened the door and watched the kid climb in, then looked back at her, those eyes killing her all over again.

"Thank your mama again for dinner. And tell Landon I'll pick him up around eight-thirty."

She waved to them as he pulled out of her driveway, then wheeled back up the ramp and into the house. From the kitchen as Dorelle cleaned—she'd shooed Mallory out when she'd tried to help—came vintage country music. Patsy Cline or some such. Twangy and angsty and not at all what Mallory wanted to hear right now. So she went down the hall to Landon's room, where he was lying flat on his back, a paperback book over his head as he read.

"Zach's picking you up at eight-thirty tomorrow morning to go with him."

"Oh, yeah?" Still holding the book aloft, he turned his head and grinned at her. "Cool."

Silence shuddered between them for several seconds. They both knew this was about more than a sudden interest in animal husbandry, but no way was she getting up in the kid's grill about it. She and Zach were going to have to work out whatever they needed to work out. Especially since she had no more idea what was going on in Zach's head than she did her son's. And yes, that aggravated her control issues out the wazoo. But whatchagonna do?

Then she said, "You know you can talk to me about anything, right?"

The book lowered to his chest. "Um…yeah?"

"Well. Okay. Wanted to make sure we were clear on that."

"We are. It's all good, Mom. I swear." Then he lifted

the book over his head again, signaling the end of the conversation.

God help her, her mother was singing along with Patsy when Mallory got to the kitchen. Only Dorelle couldn't sing to save her soul, so that was a problem. For Mallory, anyway. Clearly not Dorelle. Although when she saw Mallory, she stopped singing, shut the dishwasher and parked one hand on her hip, and Mallory decided she'd take the singing, any day.

"What?" she said, wheeling to the fridge for a bottle of water. "Or should I say, what now?"

"Other than those looks you and Zach were giving each other were like to set the table on fire? Nothing."

"They were not. Jeez, Mama, give me some credit—"

"You really don't think I know what happened between you two when you went down to Corrales? Not that I'm criticizing," she said, pressing one hand to her chest. "Far from it. In fact, let me be the first to sing, *Hallelujah*." Which she did, in a warbly soprano that made Edgar roll his eyes at Mallory. *Make it stop? Please?* "But I'm also guessing doing the deed solved nothing?"

Mallory took a long swig of her water, then twisted the cap back on the bottle. "What makes you think," she said in a low voice, "it was supposed to *solve* anything?"

"So you admit it?"

"I'm thirty-eight, for cripes' sake—"

"Hence the hallelujah…ing. Oh, baby—"

"And you have clearly forgotten how fast I can take my booty out of here. Mama," she said over her mother's huff, "this was about…getting out of the damn starting gate. Not making it to the finish line."

Mama crossed her arms. "So you're telling me you—*you*, of all people—are okay with only running part of the race?"

She shrugged. "I've mellowed." Her mother snorted.

"Then how's about I've learned to play the hand I've been given? Since it's not like I had much choice in that, did I?"

"Oooh…" Mama's eyes got all soft, which in turn softened something inside Mallory, and…crap. "You're in love with him, aren't you?"

Willing her eyes to stop stinging, Mallory tapped the bottle against her knee for a moment, then met her mother's gaze. "You remember when I was up for that role in an amazing movie a few years back? How much I wanted that part, would've killed for it, even? But I didn't get it. And, yeah, I was disappointed—"

"Russell said you cried for a week."

"Okay, so extremely disappointed. But I got over it. And then came *the* part, the one I got the Oscar for. Which I couldn't've taken if the other role hadn't fallen through. Things work out…" Dammit. She stopped. Swallowed. "Things work out the way they're supposed to. And how I feel about Zach doesn't change the fact that he's not ready to move forward. That *he's* the one who can't, or won't, finish the race—"

"He told you that?"

"Not in those words, obviously, but yes. Many, many times. But even if he hadn't, the eyes don't lie. So you know what? I've decided to be grateful for his friendship, that he makes me laugh, that…he made me feel beautiful, and worthy, and worshipped. That he sees *this*," she said, pressing a hand to her heart, before sweeping it across her legs. "Not these. And in any case…"

She glanced back toward the hallway leading to the bedrooms before meeting her mother's gaze again. "Right now, it's all about Landon. What he needs. And until I get that figured out—assuming I ever do—what *I* want comes a distant second."

For once, her mother seemed at a loss for words. But underneath the kitchen's pot lights, her eyes glistened before she closed the few feet between then to bend over, pulling Mallory's head to her chest. "What on earth did I do to get such a dear, sweet, brave daughter?"

And Mallory sighed and held her mother tight. Because sometimes, you just needed your Mama. No matter how old you got.

Or how much she sometimes drove you stark raving bonkers.

"So how come I can't go with you and Landon?"

"Because you have school," Zach said to Jeremy in a reasonably reasonable voice, considering how little sleep he'd gotten the night before. In fact, they'd gotten out the door too late to avoid the school buses now clogging the school's drop-off lane, spewing forth the kids who lived out in the sticks. They moved forward a whole three feet.

"I could skip it for one day," Jeremy said around a bite of the breakfast burrito they'd picked up from Annie's. A rare treat, but one Zach readily indulged on those days when breakfast from the diner *was* getting it together. "Nobody would care."

"I would. And no, you don't get a vote."

"That's what Mom used to say," Jeremy said, and Zach's heart twisted. He looked over at his oldest son, the new jeans he'd bought not two months before already threadbare on the knees. And too short. Making a mental note to get some new clothes for his growing child in the not-too-distant future, Zach looked back out the windshield.

"You remember that?"

"Yeah," Jeremy said, like it was no big deal. "I could get out here, you don't have to wait—"

"And incur the wrath of Mrs. Aguilar?" he said, nodding toward the down-vest-armored crossing guard who'd been ensuring the safety of Whispering Pines' youngest since Zach and his brothers were kids. "No way. Besides, it's not like I can move around the traffic, anyway." Although more was the pity on that count. Propping his wrist on the steering wheel, he tapped the gas again to move forward another inch. "So you liked Landon, huh?"

"Uh-huh. Mainly because he didn't treat me like I was some dumb little kid."

"That's because you aren't."

"Yeah, well, tell that to the big kids."

Zach almost smiled, remembering the grief he and Colin gave the twins when they were younger. Then he frowned. "Anybody being mean to you?"

Jeremy shook his head, which this frosty morning was swallowed up in a brightly colored superhero beanie at total odds with his olive drab jacket—his pick—and pumpkin-colored hoodie. "Nah, mostly they act like we don't exist." He reached up to scratch his forehead under the hat's cuff. "So it was nice, that Landon wasn't like that."

"I suppose so." *Aaand* they were almost there. "But you know he's going back to LA, right?"

The boy twisted in his seat, making the hat slip down almost over his eyes. "I bet if you married his mom he'd stay."

"That's not happening, buddy," Zach said once his throat unlocked, sending up a short, but pithy, *Why now, God?* "And before you ask, for many reasons I can't go into right now." Out of the corner of his eye—because he'd lose it if he faced the kid right now—he saw Jeremy clamp shut his mouth. "But the main one is, they're only visiting. Mallory, and her mom, and Landon…they don't really live here."

"Then why'd they buy the horses?"

"Plenty of part-timers own horses and stable them elsewhere when they're not in residence. Waffles and Macy will stay at the Vista."

"How can people live in two places? I don't get it."

At least that made Zach smile. "Some people have houses all over the world. So they spend a few months here, a few months there…" He shrugged. "It works for them."

"Well, that's just nuts," Jeremy muttered, grabbing his backpack off the floor as they finally pulled into the drop-off zone and the kid undid his seat belt. But before he got out, he twisted around to give Zach a hug, something he imagined would get knocked off the checklist before too much longer. Then he leaned back and said, "So maybe we could go live in LA. Wherever the heck that is," before pushing open the door and disappearing into the swarm of short people trekking toward the school's entrance.

His head spinning, Zach pulled out of the loop and back onto the road, half tempted to call Mallory and re-nege on the offer to let Landon ride shotgun this morning. Between last night's conversation and his son's "sugges-tion" he wasn't sure he was up for whatever *her* son was about to lay on him.

Not to mention he wasn't sure he wanted to see her right now.

Because he did. Way too much. All that stuff she said about him being special, simply for doing what needed doing…

But he didn't call, didn't back out, didn't turn and run as if a pissed-off bull was on his tail. Because the other stuff she'd said? About facing her fears?

Yeah. That.

Mallory wheeled out onto the porch behind Landon, grabbing his hand before he could zip away, and Zach's breath clogged in his lungs so hard it hurt. But it wasn't her beauty threatening to derail his self-control, although the way the sun tangled with her hair definitely made him dry-mouthed. And let's not even get into what her smile was doing to him. But far more than those, it was her *spirit*, her honesty and strength and generosity that shook him up so much he could barely think straight.

Not to mention her courage.

Fine, so maybe he'd helped her unlock, or rediscover, or whatever, her confidence enough for her to finally face whatever demons still lurked up at the resort. And absolutely, Zach was proud of her. But damned if he was about to take credit for what had always been there. And once she realized that, she'd have even less reason to hang around.

However, if he'd learned anything in life, it was that telling somebody something—especially if that somebody was female—before they were ready to hear it rarely ended well. For anybody. People simply had to come to these conclusions in their own good time, and without what would surely be considered outside interference.

So he'd take the boy up to the Vista, say whatever it came to him to say, and try his hardest not to think about how pretty and smart and kind his mama was and how much Zach was gonna miss her when she left. Even if that was best for all parties concerned.

His heart pounding, Zach lowered the window, trying to act like none of this was any big deal when it was all a *very* big deal. And everyone here knew it.

"You ready?" he said to the boy, who nodded, then grudgingly bestowed a peck on his mother's cheek before tromping over to the truck and getting in, emitting what could only be described as a stench of distrust.

"Have fun!" Mallory called out, and Landon grunted something in reply as he latched his seat belt, and then they were on their way, one obviously tormented adolescent and the man who was the cause of the torment.

But not for long, Zach hoped.

* * *

Now that he was alone with Zach, Landon realized he had no idea what to say, or ask, or anything.

"There's food in the bag," Zach said mildly, nodding toward a huge white bag at Landon's feet. "Didn't know what you liked, so I got a selection."

Landon had actually already eaten a bowl of cereal, but the smells coming from that bag were making his stomach growl like crazy. So he pulled it up on his lap and dug through. Something that looked like a long, skinny doughnut with cinnamon sugar. A takeout carton with scrambled eggs. A tortilla wrapped around more scrambled eggs and bacon and potatoes, he thought. A fruit cup, which was sorta lame, but he supposed some people liked it. A couple bottles of OJ.

"Which one do you want?" he asked, hoping Zach would say the fruit cup. Or the plain scrambled eggs.

"I already ate, take whatever you like."

"You sure?"

"I'm sure. Really."

"Okay. Thanks." He took out the skinny doughnut thing, frowning at it. "What is this?"

"A churro. Traditional Mexican dessert, but works for breakfast, too."

Cinnamon sugar rained all over Landon's front as he took his first bite of the chewy pastry. "This is really good," he said around a full mouth.

"Gotta warn you though, they're addictive," Zach said, and Landon giggled. And took another bite as he looked every-which-way out the truck's windows, at the flat gold landscape on one side, the mountains on the other, the deep blue sky. It wasn't like he'd never seen blue sky before— they'd traveled and stuff—but this looked unreal. Still chewing, he frowned, trying to find the right words to describe it.

"The sky…"

"Yeah?"

"It's like…when I take a breath? I feel like I'm breathing it in."

Zach shot him a grin. "Never thought of it like that. But you're right." He breathed in himself, slowly let it out. "That's exactly it."

Licking his fingers, Landon opened the bag again. Was it weird, how okay he felt with somebody he'd basically just met? Or maybe that's the way stuff was supposed to work, who knew? "What's the thing with all the stuff inside?"

"A breakfast burrito."

"Right. I knew that. You sure I can have it?"

"Knock yourself out."

It was even better than the churro. Dang. But before he'd swallowed his first bite, Zach said, "I'm guessing this little trip is about more than you wanting to be a vet." He glanced over. "Am I right?" Landon sighed, and Zach sort of laughed. "Hey. It's up to you whether or not you want to talk about whatever's bugging you. But you'll probably feel better if you do. And I probably will, too. You've got questions about me and your mother, don't you?"

Landon wrapped up the uneaten part of the burrito and stuffed it back in the bag, crunching it closed before looking at Zach's profile. "Are you two going together?"

Zach took longer to answer than Landon would've liked. "The last thing I want to do is make you think I'm avoiding your question, but the thing is…" Frowning, he shot another glance Landon's way. "It's no secret I like your mother. A lot." He looked back out the windshield. "Maybe even more than a lot. But to be honest, there's more reasons why things wouldn't work out between us than reasons why they could. Or might."

Not at all what he'd expected. "What sorts of reasons?"

"Well, for starters," Zach said quietly, "it hasn't been

that long since my wife died. The boys' mother?" Landon nodded. "So I'm not really ready for another relationship. Not a serious one, anyway. And for another, this is my home. Where I belong. Where my practice is. My family. And your mother and you…you're not staying in Whispering Pines. Right?"

Landon frowned harder. "No, I suppose not."

"So there you are. But probably the most important reason is…" Another glance. "You."

"Me?"

"That's right, you. Because seems to me you've gone through enough changes in the last little while, you don't need any more. And I know your mama feels the same way. So if you're worried I'm gonna do something to bring any more upheaval into your life…" He shook his head. "You can rest easy on that score."

"And grown-ups have lied to me before." Rats. His face got all hot. "I'm sorry," he muttered. "I didn't mean—"

"I would never lie to you, Landon," Zach said, not sounding mad at all. "For all the reasons I just said." He glanced over. "I swear. However…" He took a deep breath. "If I'm way off base here, feel free to ignore me. But is there something you need to tell your mother?"

"Why? What'd she say?"

"Only that she senses you're not being completely open with her. About what, though, she doesn't know."

Before he even knew the words were there, Landon said, "I don't want to worry her. Not after…well. You know."

"She's a mother, worrying is a major part of the job description. But I'll tell you something else—and this is from only knowing her for a few weeks—your mama is one of the toughest people I've ever met. What she went through…it didn't make her weaker. It made her stronger. And I guarantee you she can handle whatever you tell her. What she *can't* handle, is not knowing what's going on." He briefly met Landon's gaze. "You understand what I'm saying?"

Since his throat refused to work, he nodded. Zach glanced over. "It's gonna be okay, bud," he said, his voice soft. "Because your mother loves you like nobody's business."

Landon sucked in a breath, as if trying to absorb strength from the sky. "I know." He tried to smile over at Zach, but it felt all tight. "Thanks."

"No problem. And by the way? It's easy to see why your mother's so proud of you. You're obviously a pretty incredible kid, putting her feelings ahead of your own."

His face prickled all over again. Especially since he had the feeling Zach didn't say stuff just to say it. In fact, in some ways this conversation had gone a whole lot better than he'd thought it would. In others, however...

He remembered what Mom had said last night. About how he could tell her anything.

Then he looked out his window so Zach wouldn't see him cry.

After briefly filling Mallory in on his trip—which had apparently involved feeling a colt underneath its mama's ribs and a ride on another mare—Landon had disappeared into his room. Zach had told her later, on the phone, that they'd "talked," although he seemed no more inclined to share the details than her son. Now, however, as she sat on the deck taking in the last rays of the setting sun while her mother got dinner ready, Landon joined her, plopping in a nearby chair in a position only possible to snakes and eleven-year-old boys. He'd always had his pensive moods, even as a baby, but now the poor kid looked as if he bore the entire weight of the world on his still-slight shoulders.

Figuring the opening salvo needed to be his, Mallory

wrapped her shawl more tightly around her shoulders and waited. Finally Landon looked over at her, his slender face marred by a scowl that would've been comical had the confusion in his eyes not incinerated her heart.

"What is it, honey?" she said, gently prodding, and the kid dragged in a breath.

"Zach said I shouldn't keep stuff from you."

And her heart melted a little more. "Which is kind of what I said, too, if you recall."

"I know. But…" He pushed out a huge sigh. And then, his chin wobbling like the big boy who really, really didn't want to cry, he came clean about what the last few weeks had really been like.

"Oh, honey…" Mallory breathed when he was done. Angry and heartbroken—but mostly angry—she opened her arms for him to come sit on her lap, where she wrapped him up close like he was Liam's age again, realizing her time here—in Whispering Pines, with Zach—was up.

And *heartbroken* edged out the anger.

Chapter Twelve

Shortly after ten that night, Zach's cell rang. Setting his cup of coffee on the table in front of him, he frowned at the display...until he realized who it was.

"Sorry to call so late," Mallory said quickly, whispering. "I had to wait until Landon passed out."

"No problem," Zach said, almost as quietly, since in the tiny house voices carried as if they were amplified. He could go outside, but if the way the juniper branches scratched at the window was any indication he'd never be able to hear her. Not to mention he'd freeze. "What's up?"

"Landon talked."

Asleep beside him on the sofa, Benny grunted when Zach leaned forward. "Oh, yeah?"

"Don't get me wrong, I'm grateful—so grateful—that whatever you said did the trick. But now I feel like a complete idiot."

"Why—?"

"Most of the time, I like to think I'm a reasonably aware

person. And it's not as if I didn't know I was the more involved parent. After all, I wanted a baby, and Russell conceded, but…" She pushed out a breath. "I thought—or maybe I just wanted to believe—that after the accident he'd step up his game. Because for a while there I couldn't be Mom. In my heart, yes, of course, but… I simply c-couldn't. *Any*way—"

Zach could almost see her slice the air in front of her, making herself regain her composure. "It was Russell's suggestion, actually, that I take a break, let the paparazzi find some other target to circle. So I figured Russell would, you know, pick up the slack? Be the kid's frickin' *father*, for God's sake? But, no."

The old retriever shifted to lay his head on Zach's knee. "What on earth happened?"

"Apparently the new Mrs. Eames isn't all that into being a stepmom. Not full-time, anyway. Nor was Russell into being a full-time father, apparently. The duties of which he handily relegated to our old housekeeper. Who's fabulous, don't get me wrong, but she's not our child's *mother*. Turns out, most weekends, they were gone. Most *nights*, they were gone."

"You're kidding?"

"Nope. Russell would check in on him for a few minutes at breakfast, and then Landon was lucky if he saw him again that night."

Anger heating his face, Zach glanced down the hall, where his own two little boys were safely tucked in their beds. "I assume you've handed your ex's head to him on a platter?"

"Working up to it. But the way I feel right now? The man'll be lucky to get it back in a Walmart bag."

Zach almost smiled, then sighed. "Why on earth didn't Landon say something to you?" Although no sooner were the words out of his mouth than he knew the answer.

"Because—get this—he didn't want to worry me. Because I'd been through enough and he didn't want to pile on top of it. Can you believe it? The kid's *eleven*. If I'd had *any* idea…"

"But you didn't, honey," Zach said, wishing he could see her. Touch her. "If Landon didn't tell you—"

"And while we were in Corrales," she said, her voice strained, even as he could *feel* her shaking through the phone, "my *child* was basically left alone in some huge house eight hundred miles away."

The guilt and torment in her voice shredded him. Zach thought of Heidi, how fiercely she'd loved her babies, and how much that love had made him love her more. Now, hearing Mallory, all he wanted was to wrap his arms around her, reassure her she'd done nothing wrong.

Even as he realized he'd never get that chance.

"So you're going back with him."

A long pause preceded, "We may as well stay out the week. I still have places I want to show him. And I'm not giving up the house. Or the horses. I don't think. But… yes." He heard her pull in a breath. "I can handle it now. All of it. It's like…" He heard a dry chuckle. "I found my footing again. Thanks in no small part to you."

Zach tried a laugh. "And there you go again—"

"Because it's true. I honestly believed, when I came out here, I was thinking primarily of my son. Now I realize… it wasn't Landon I was trying to shield nearly as much as I was trying to protect myself."

"From?"

"The truth," she said after a moment. "That I had no idea what my purpose was anymore. A fact only confirmed with every camera flash, every pathetic pic that showed up on some supermarket rag. I still don't know, frankly. What I do know is that I need to be with my son. And the paparazzi can go screw themselves."

Even as he smiled, her words slammed into him like a sledgehammer.

"You're saying goodbye."

"We both knew this was coming, Zach," she said gently. "That this…was an interlude. One you'd better believe I'll never forget. But my place isn't here. Not now. And your place isn't anywhere else. Even if…even if you were free. Which you know you're not."

That he couldn't refute her words nearly killed him. But she was right.

"Will I see you before you leave?"

Silence yawned between them. "The polite Southern girl in me says that's up to you," she finally said. "The control freak, however, doesn't think that's a good idea. I will say one thing, though, because I promised myself to be more honest. To be better about saying what's in my heart instead of what I think people want to hear. So from my heart, Zachary Talbot—thank you for letting me love you. Even if only for this little while."

Then she disconnected the call. Zach stared at his phone for what felt like an eternity before finally heaving himself to his feet and pocketing it. Feeling like he was in a dream, he found his way to his kitchen to warm up his cold, nasty cup of coffee. He opened the microwave, set the cup on the turntable. Told himself this was all for the best, really. That Landon had opened up and Mallory had figured out how to fix her broken child before it was too late…

That she was leaving before Zach could break her. Or at least her heart.

He slammed shut the microwave door so hard the poor dog looked up at him with a *What the hell, man?* look on his face.

The slight creak in the hallway by her bedroom door made Mallory turn her head. Mama stood there, her expression one big question.

"Guess I'll call Josh in the morning," Mallory said,

"about boarding the horses. At least until I can figure out whether to bring 'em out to board someplace closer to home—" the word caught in her throat "—or sell 'em."

"You don't have to decide anything right away, baby."

"True."

"You okay?" Mama said softly.

"I will be."

Her arms folded across her ribs, her mother simply stood there for a long moment before at last she nodded. "I'll be up for a while yet, if you need me."

"Thanks. But I'm good."

"'Night, baby."

"'Night."

Finally alone again, Mallory blew out a huge sigh, then went about the tediousness of getting ready for bed. Usually she didn't even think about her old life, where going to bed meant simply stripping off her clothes and climbing under the covers. Tonight, however, every labored movement, every stretch and push and pull and grunt reminded her of what she'd lost.

What she'd almost had.

Finally, nightgown on and teeth brushed, she transferred to her bed, where she propped pillows behind her back, and a book she knew she'd never be able to concentrate on on her dead legs.

Time. That was all she'd wanted.

To give Zach the room he needed for his brain to catch up to his heart. Or whatever it was that made him look at her the way he did. Make love to her the way he had. Yeah, he was a nice guy and all, but the things he'd done for her…the way he'd made her feel…

She wasn't that delusional. Was she?

Even though nobody knew better than she did—these days, anyway—that you couldn't simply *will* things to work out the way you wanted them to. That sometimes, dedication to a goal wasn't enough, if timing and luck and other factors outside your control weren't lined up in your favor.

That loving somebody, even with all your heart, wasn't enough to break through the fear holding theirs prisoner. Not to mention give up their life to make a new one with you.

The book slammed shut and thunked onto her nightstand, Mallory twisted around to turn off the light, then shoved herself down underneath the covers and over onto her side, stuffing a pillow between her knees to keep the pressure sores at bay. She knew she was doing the right thing, that Landon came first. That wasn't even a question. But for a little while she'd allowed herself to live in a dream world of her own making, one where the heroine absolutely got her happy-ever-after.

Too bad she couldn't pull a spoiled-actress hissy fit and demand the ending be rewritten.

Seriously.

"Hello? Where is everybody?"

Sudsed up beyond all recognition, Jeremy twisted around in the bathtub, sending a tsunami crashing over the edge and across Zach, on his knees beside the tub. Not to mention his little brother, who blinked, gasped and broke into a belly laugh.

"In here, Gran!" the kid bellowed. So much for Zach's eardrums. A second later—because none of them had a lick of shame—his mother appeared at the bathroom door, draped in some blanket-like thing and sporting what Zach guessed were the world's oldest pair of lined boots. She held first one bulging, reusable tote. "Clothes we've accumulated over the past month—" then another "—and food. Because I'm your mother, that's why, so don't argue."

Zach gave her a wan smile. "Wasn't going to."

"Look what I can do, Gran!" With that, Liam grabbed his nose and disappeared under a foot of froth floating on six inches of water. A second later, he came up, grinning, dripping red curls sparkling with a million tiny, iridescent bubbles.

"Just like your father," Zach's mother said, chuckling. "You all wrinkly yet?" she said, grabbing a towel off the rack, and the toddler frowned at his pruny fingers.

"Yep." He held out his hands for inspection. "See?"

"Then come here, baby, let me dry you off."

Zach steadied the dripping, slippery little boy as he climbed out, then handed him to his grandmother before wrapping Jeremy up in another towel, briskly drying the boy's hair as his teeth chattered.

"This was always one of my favorite times, you know," Mom said behind him, sitting on the closed toilet and doing the same buffing routine with his youngest. "Partly because it meant at least some of you would be asleep soon."

"Yeah," Zach said, smiling into Jeremy's eyes. "I know how that goes."

Although truth be told, he didn't look forward to the boys' going to bed the way he once did. Because that meant being alone. Missing the sound of Mallory's voice, her laughter. The sparkle in her eyes right before she delivered a zinger.

Missing *her*.

"What I wouldn't give to be inside your head right now," Mom said, and Zach sighed.

"Trust me, that is not someplace you want to be."

After a long moment's stare, she stood, heaving Liam up with her. "Come on, you two—let's get your jammies on."

But Jeremy wrapped his still-damp self around Zach's

neck and said in his ear, "C'n I play a game for a little while? *Pleeease*?"

Zach grabbed his son, making him tumble into his lap, a giggling tangle of towel and limbs. "Only for fifteen minutes. You have school tomorrow."

"Okay," Jeremy said, wriggling free and dumping the wet towel in a heap behind him before running naked down the hall to his room, yelling at the top of his lungs the whole way.

"That, I don't miss," his mother muttered, then tickled Liam, igniting another giggle fit. "How about I put you to bed tonight?"

"Only if you read me books."

"Deal. How many?"

The baby held up both hands, fingers splayed. "This many!"

"Two," Zach said, straightening out the bathroom.

"You heard the man," Mom said, starting out of the room, only to turn around and say, "And you, I'll meet in the living room after."

Of course.

He'd actually dozed off sitting on the sofa when he felt his mother's not-so-gentle prod. Jerking awake, he blinked at her as she plopped in the chair across from him. "Liam's passed out, Jer's reading in his bed."

"Thanks," Zach said, yawning, trying not to notice she'd crossed her arms in her now-we're-gonna-talk position.

"So I ran into Dorelle in the grocery store today. She said they were all going back to LA on Saturday."

Not looking at his mother, Zach leaned forward to link his hands between his knees. "Apparently Landon's dad isn't exactly hands-on. Which Mallory didn't fully realize until the kid told her."

"So I gather." His mother paused. "You know, they

need vets there, too. For all those frou-frou little dogs and what-not."

Zach laughed. Sort of. "I can't move to California, Mom."

"Because...?"

"Because my life is here?"

She snorted. "And half a life's no better than none. It's time you stop making excuses and accept the damn gift, already. Don't you look at me like that, you know as well as I do you're crazy about that sweet woman. And from what Dorelle tells me, she's pretty crazy about you, too. Or maybe just crazy, I don't know."

His heart was beating so hard it hurt. "Except..." He blew out a breath. "Dammit, Mom, I don't want—"

"What? To be loved again? Or to let yourself love? Because either way that definitely makes you the crazy one. And in any case, it's too late."

"To stop her from going back? Like I don't know that?"

And judging from his mother's sly smile, he'd definitely played his hand there.

"No, goofball. Too late to convince me or anyone else you don't love her. Not after everything you've done. And I'll leave you to fill in the blanks on that one. And please do not tell me you were only being neighborly or friendly or whatever the hell excuse you plan on throwing out there. I *know* you, honey," she said, her voice softening. "I know what you look like when you've lost your heart. What I'm afraid of this time, is that if you don't go after this? You'll lose your soul, too. And for your boys' sakes, if nothing else...don't let that happen."

She stood, gathering her purse and keys from the table by the front door, shrouding herself in that wrap. "I loved Heidi with my whole heart, because I could see how much she loved you. And I know the last thing she'd want, is to see you stuck like this. To be afraid of *living* again."

Mom came back to the sofa, but only long enough to

bend over and plant a quick kiss on the top of his head. Then she took his chin in her hand. "For the past two years you've shown your sons what courage is. And your father and I couldn't be more proud of you. But I swear, if you drop the ball on this, I will take an ad out in the *Whispering Pines Gazette* telling the whole world what a jackass my son is."

At that, Zach had to laugh. "Or at least the twenty-two people who actually read the thing."

"Word travels," she said, and swooped out the front door, the cold breeze left in her wake making the drapes on the picture window in front of him shudder.

He was pissed, of course. Although because she'd interfered, or because she was right, he wasn't sure. Because, hell, yeah, he was in love with Mallory. Had been from within ten minutes of meeting her, if he was being honest. That wasn't the problem. The problem was…what if he couldn't shake the fear?

Zach leaned forward, his head in his hands.

What if, what if, what if…?

His head shot up, a frown the size of the Grand Canyon biting into his forehead as it hit him… Mallory wasn't nearly as paralyzed as he was.

And if he wanted to keep his man card, he'd better damn sight do something about that.

The week had gone by way too fast. Because the day after tomorrow he and Mom and Grandma were going back to LA. And then what?

Sitting up on Waffles, Landon watched his mother saddle up Macy, wheeling from one side of the horse to the other to tighten the cinch. They'd gone riding every day, even if only for a little while, and he was getting a lot better at not feeling like he was gonna slip off. But watching Mom, seeing how confident she was even when she couldn't really feel the horse underneath her—that was something. Except even though she smiled and laughed, and he believed her when she said she was glad he'd told her the truth, he could tell, by the way she'd sit on the deck and watch the sunset, or roll out to the pasture to talk to the horses, she was really going to miss it here.

And he kinda felt like it was all his fault, even when he knew that was stupid. The worst thing, though, was that he'd thought Mom had bought this place for keeps, so they could come back any time they wanted. But last night, he'd heard Mom and Grandma talking about maybe selling the house. It was insane, how much he loved it here, too, even after only a week. Not to mention how much he loved Waffles, dumb name and all. He could do without having to wear a riding helmet, but Mom said he had to, until he was a stronger rider.

"How you doing over there?" Mom asked, sitting up real straight in the saddle, wearing a seat-belt-like thing to help keep her balanced. They'd followed a path that went up into the forest, a few gold leaves hanging on to the mostly bare trees crammed in between the pines. You could see the mountains great from here. And the sky. And down below, a river cutting through the landscape, sparkling like a giant silver snake.

"Pretty good. I think I've got the hang of it now."

"Definitely getting there. Although when we get back, how about getting you some real lessons?"

"Like barrel racing and stuff? Like you did?"

"If you want to, sure. Why not?"

He didn't ask if that meant they'd take the horses with them, or have somebody bring them out. Because he didn't think he was ready for the answer, if she said no. They rode in silence for a few more minutes until Landon said, "So how come Zach and the boys haven't come over again?"

"Oh. You know." Mom kept looking straight ahead, like she was concentrating on where the horse was going. Although it was obvious the horse had this. "People get busy."

"But he knows we're leaving, right?"

"Uh-huh."

"Don't you think that's kind of weird? I mean, you guys are friends and stuff, right?"

Now Mom gave him a funny look. "You liked him, didn't you?"

"Well, yeah. Why wouldn't I? He's pretty cool. And he was really nice to me."

She glanced away again. "Zach's really nice to everybody."

"No," Landon said slowly, feeling his forehead pinch. "I mean, yeah, I know he's nice to everybody, but…" He sighed. "He made me feel like I was important. Like when he was talking to me he was really talking to *me*. *To* me, not at me."

When he looked over at Mom, her eyes were all shiny. "I know what you mean," she said. "But you were only with him for a few hours."

"Sometimes that's all you need to know somebody's your friend, right?"

"That's very true, kiddo." She faced front again. "Very true. So, speaking of friends…who're you going to call when you get back home?"

Home. Funny how you could live in one place all your life and yet after one week someplace else…

Landon sighed. They'd gone to see the Indian ruins and Santa Fe, up to the ski resort and sometimes no place in particular, just driving around. It was quiet out here. Almost spooky, sometimes, especially at night—he hadn't realized how much LA kind of hummed all the time. But mostly, it was peaceful.

And you could actually breathe the air. You could actually *breathe*—

"Landon?"

"Oh. Sorry. I don't know yet—"

Mom's phone buzzed. Holding up one finger, she dug it out of her jacket pocket, frowning at the screen. She typed a short reply and shoved it back. "That was Grandma," she said, sounding confused. "Zach and the boys are over at the house."

"Really?"

She nodded, then tugged at the reins to turn her horse around. "Guess we should get back."

The trail got too narrow for them to ride side by side, so Landon rode behind Mom. But that was okay, because this way she couldn't see his grin...

It'd taken a while to settle the horses and get back to the house, during which Mallory's brain came *this close* to burning up. However, by the time her mother swept the three boys off to heaven knew where, she'd finally convinced herself the man had simply come to say goodbye. Even though she'd told him not to. A thought that got her brain fizzing all over again.

Especially when she saw his face.

Zach stood in the middle of the living room in a barn coat and jeans, his fingers crushing his cowboy hat's curled-up brim.

"I can't let you leave without telling you how I feel," he said, and her knees would've buckled if they could've done such a thing.

"O-oh?"

"Yeah," he pushed out, scrunching up the brim even worse. "Because..." He cleared his throat. "All that you said, about how I pushed you past your fears? Well, I guess I could say you did the same thing for me. To me.

Whatever." When she didn't say anything—because she couldn't—he cleared his throat again and said, "To be honest, I didn't want to fall in love with you. With anybody, for that matter. Because…" She saw his throat work. "Because it hurt too much, losing Heidi. Except…"

His eyes glittered behind his glasses, making Mallory's water, too. "Corrales wouldn't've happened if I hadn't, whether I wanted to admit that to myself or not. Then, when it really sank in you were leaving, that I might not ever see you again, I realized how stupid it was trying to keep myself from getting hurt again. Since it'd happened anyway."

"Oh, Zach…"

"No, wait, I'm not finished. So long story short, I've been doing some research online, and it looks like I wouldn't have any trouble finding work in LA. And the boys are young enough I don't think the transition would be any big deal. Not sure what I'd do about housing. I know it's off-the-wall expensive out there, but… I'll figure it out." He removed his glasses to skim a thumb under his right eye, pushed the glasses back on. "Because I have to. Because while losing Heidi was something I couldn't control, losing you…that'd be nobody's fault but mine."

Their gazes locked, it occurred to Mallory that despite Zach's still standing several feet away, what now vibrated between them was more real, more palpable, than anything a lousy bunch of nerve endings could ever communicate. But for all she ached to accept what he was offering, pragmatism still raised its ugly head.

"And I love you far too much to let you make that kind of sacrifice for me," she said quietly. "Because suppose this doesn't work out? We barely know each other, for heaven's sake. Yes, I'm sure the kids would adjust, kids are good at that, but…would you? I doubt it. What I don't doubt, is that you'd be miserable in LA. Even more a fish out of water than I was." She smiled. "Which is saying a lot—"

"I'm a big boy, Mallory, I can make my own decisions—"

"No," she said, finally wheeling closer, "now you listen to *me*— I know exactly how much you love it here. How much you belong. Know, because I feel the same way about this place. And how could you leave your family? Yes, we could come back for visits, of course, but it wouldn't be the same. And there is no way I could live with myself, taking that from you—"

"But what if we stayed here?" Landon said from the doorway, making Mallory swivel around to face him.

"Landon! What on earth—!"

"No, really," the boy said, coming closer, looking more scared, and more determined, than Mallory had ever seen him. "What if I said I didn't want to go back to LA? Not to live, anyway. Really, think about it—Dad clearly doesn't care, and he's going to Brazil on location for six months to shoot that movie, anyway. Didn't he tell you?"

Mallory heaved a sigh. "No, he did not."

With that, Landon's gaze swung to Zach, then back to Mallory. "Okay, maybe you don't see it, but I do—Dad never looked at you the way Zach does. Not even before you guys got divorced." She saw him swallow. "He never looked at me, either, the way Zach does. Like, you know, he actually *sees* me?" He turned back to Zach. "Like... like he gets me."

Slowly, Zach smiled. "Thank you."

"You're welcome," Landon said, then faced Mallory again. "See, Mom? This is a good thing. You really need to go for it."

Feeling as if her chest was about to cave in, Mallory released a long breath, only to startle slightly when she felt Zach's lovely strong hands cup her shoulders from behind. She reached up to close her fingers over his, her heart melting into a big ol' puddle of goo. But…

"What about school?"

Zach chuckled. "We have them here. Well, one. But it works."

"And I can always do extra stuff online, if I want," Landon put in. "And Josh said he'd let me come work at the ranch any time I wanted. To learn more about horses and stuff. Please, Mom?" he whispered. "Can we stay?"

At that, Zach squatted beside her, taking her hand in both of his so she had to look into his eyes, the corners all crinkled as he smiled. "And FYI? Whatever you decide, you're not getting rid of me. Because we belong together."

What she couldn't decide, was whether to smack him or kiss him. "But how on earth do you know that? After only a few weeks?"

"I just do," he said, his eyes soft, and with that, so did she.

With great effort, Mallory hauled her gaze away from the only man she really, truly-ever-after loved and said to her son, "Then, unless your father puts up a stink—which I'm guessing isn't an issue—yes. We'll stay." At the kid's fist pump, she smiled. "Now go away so Zach and I can finish our discussion—"

"One more question," he said, and she burped out a little laugh.

"Yes?"

"Can we bring the dogs out here? To live with us?"

"Oh, honey…of course."

"Yes!" he said, then bounced out of the room, barely gone two seconds before Zach scooped Mallory out of the chair.

"Zach! What on earth are you doing?"

"This," he said, sinking into the cushy leather sofa with

her on his lap a moment before his mouth claimed hers.
For a really long time.

A really, *really* long time.

Then, before they passed out from lack of oxygen, she
skimmed her fingers through his hair and said, "There's
still an awful lot to sort out, you know. Like what I'm going
to do with the LA house. What I'm going to do with myself, here all the time. Because I'm not sure riding Macy
and making love with you is gonna cut it. As idyllic as that
sounds." Zach grinned. "And I don't actually know what
Russell's reaction will be—"

"To our getting married, you mean?"

Her fingers laced around the back of his neck, Mallory
jerked. "You're not serious."

"It's okay, I don't mean tomorrow. Not that I would
object. But I do realize the kids need time to get to know
each other. To get used to the idea of being brothers."

"Not to mention me getting used to the idea of being
your wife."

He shrugged. "Sure."

"Wow." Then, slowly, a smile stretched across her face.
"Oh. Wow…"

"I take it that's a yes?"

"That's an *oh, hell*, yes," she said, and he laughed and
kissed her again, and she felt whole, and perfect, and
loved, as she never had before.

Hallelujah, was right.

Epilogue

A few weeks later...

"How do I look?"

Pouring the last bag of sugar rush fuel into a plastic bowl, Zach turned around in his kitchen and nearly had a heart attack. Although he had to admit, with her red hair teased and sprayed out to kingdom come and her wicked, wicked grin, Mallory made the best damn zombie he'd ever seen.

"Freaking awesome," he said, just as Landon rounded the corner from the hallway in his Transmutant costume and burst out laughing.

"Holy crud, Mom—the little kids'll wet their pants."

"Yeah? Cool." She wheeled over and grabbed a miniature chocolate bar out of the dish, unwrapped it and poked it into her mouth. Black, of course. To match the black circles around her eyes. "Because I live for scaring little kids. Hey, munchkin," she said to Liam as he wandered in, shoving aside dogs as he tugged at the seat of his ninja pants. Potty-trained at last? One could hope. Mallory held out her arms and the totally unfazed kid climbed up into her lap. She kissed his cheek, then rubbed off the black splotch she'd left behind. "You all ready to go trick-or-treating?"

"Uh-huh," he said with a vigorous nod. Although Zach doubted the tyke had a clue what any of it meant. He would have, by the end of the night, however. Zach had already planned where he'd stash the stash.

His heart melted as he watched Mallory and his son, bonded as if he'd been hers from the get-go. Jeremy, too, who absolutely adored her—in large part, Zach suspected, because she encouraged him to talk about Heidi.

Same as she did with Zach, her eyes gentle as they'd lie in bed—on those rare occasions when they could pawn the spawn off on various grandparents, that is—her head propped in her hand as she listened intently...

He turned back to his task, thinking he had more blessings to count than there were candy bars in the bowl. And dogs, he thought as Landon's Great Dane/Lab mix plopped her chin on the counter, hopeful—

"No way," Zach muttered, and the dog sighed and slunk off to plop beside Benny beside the fireplace. It was truly insane, the way things were falling into place in ways none of them could have possibly foreseen. Although Russell had blustered for about half a minute when Mallory told him Landon wanted to stay, in the end he'd conceded—more out of gratitude than grace, it seemed to Zach. There'd be visits, of course, but it was clear the man was happy to hand off full-time responsibility for his son—not to mention a trio of dogs he'd barely tolerated—to his ex-wife and her future husband. An attitude Zach couldn't even begin to fathom, but since he got another awesome kid out of the deal…well. Russell's loss, he supposed.

And Mallory had already asked Adrienne about working with her at her training facility, with an eye to perhaps establishing her own one day. She'd also decided to use her fame to start a video blog of her story—struggles, triumphs and all. So her worries about rotting away out in the boonies? Not a problem.

They hadn't set a wedding date yet. Way too early for that, they'd both agreed. In the spring, maybe. Although Dorelle—who'd gone to help Annie and AJ hand out goodies at the diner—thought they were nuts to wait. Especially since she was chomping at the bit to have three grandsons under her roof. Along with their rapidly growing menagerie. Zach hadn't yet decided what to do with the little house next to his clinic where he and Heidi had brought home their babies, but he supposed that would fall into place, too.

The bowl full, Zach carried it out to the porch and set it on a little table, then squatted to light the huge jack-o'-lantern he and the boys had carved the night before, complete with tossing pumpkin guts at each other and the poor confused dogs barking their heads off, wondering what in the blue blazes was going on. For more years than Zach even knew, the tradition was that the houses closest to the town square handed out the candy, so the kids from the surrounding ranches and the like could have the traditional trick-or-treating experience. To keep things equitable, everybody brought candy to Annie and AJ's diner, and they in turn distributed the loot to the participating residents in town. And every year, pumpkins for carving appeared like magic on people's porches the Saturday before the holiday…from the Great Pumpkin, the legend went, although the adults all knew it was Granville Blake's doing—

"Is it weird," Mallory said behind him, "that I'm looking forward to this as much as the kids? Maybe even more?"

He turned to her, smiling at her zombie rags fluttering over several layers of clothing to keep from freezing her butt off while she doled out candy and good times.

"Not at all. I'm exactly the same way."

"Oh, yeah?"

"You kidding? I live for holidays."

Or had, before Heidi's death. And now…guess that had been restored to him, too, he thought as he looked back at the quiet little street, rapidly morphing from benign to spooky as daylight gave way to flickering faces in other pumpkins, decorations bobbing eerily in the late fall breeze. A moment later, it seemed, it was dark, the full moon peeking out from behind a lone cloud. He felt Mallory's hand slip into his.

"What're you thinking?" she asked.

With another smile, Zach looked down into those beautiful, black-rimmed gray eyes. "That I'm so freaking happy I could pop."

"Right answer," she said, and he bent over to kiss her.

"I've never kissed a zombie before," he whispered.

She grinned. "First time for everything."

A second later the boys all trooped onto the porch, the older two wielding pillowcases—he wasn't sure whether they were being optimistic or greedy—while Liam clutched the handle of an old plastic pumpkin Zach thought might've been his, once upon a time.

"Well, we're off," he said, hiking Liam up into his arms. "See you later."

"Count on it," Mallory said softly, and Zach stepped off

his porch into the veritable horde of goblins and ghouls and ghosts swarming the block…

…as the ones that'd lived in his head for so long floated away into nothingness.

* * * * *

COMING NEXT MONTH FROM

HARLEQUIN®

SPECIAL EDITION

Available March 22, 2016

#2467 FORTUNE'S SPECIAL DELIVERY
The Fortunes of Texas: All Fortune's Children
by Michelle Major
British playboy Charles Fortune Chesterfield doesn't think he'll ever settle down.
That is, until he runs into a former girlfriend, Alice Meyers, whose adorable baby
looks an awful lot like him...

#2468 TWO DOCTORS & A BABY
Those Engaging Garretts!
by Brenda Harlen
Dr. Avery Wallace knows that an unplanned pregnancy will present her with many
challenges—but falling in love with Justin Garrett, her baby's father, might be the
biggest one of all!

#2469 HOW TO LAND HER LAWMAN
The Bachelors of Blackwater Lake
by Teresa Southwick
April Kennedy is tired of being the girl Will Fletcher left behind. When he fills in as
the town sheriff for the summer, she plans to make him fall for her, then dump him.
But Cupid has other plans for them both.

#2470 THE COWBOY'S DOUBLE TROUBLE
Brighton Valley Cowboys
by Judy Duarte
When rancher Braden Rayburn finds himself looking after orphaned twins, he hires
a temporary nanny, Elena Ramirez. He couldn't ever imagine they would fall for the
kids—and each other—and create the perfect family.

#2471 AN OFFICER AND HER GENTLEMAN
Peach Leaf, Texas
by Amy Woods
Army medic Avery Abbott is suffering from severe PTSD—and she needs
assistance, stat! Thanks to dog trainer Isaac Meyer and Avery's rescue pup, Foggy,
Avery may have found the healing she requires—and true love.

#2472 THE GIRL HE LEFT BEHIND
The Crandall Lake Chronicles
by Patricia Kay
When Adam Crenshaw returns to Crandall Lake, Eve Kelly can't help but wonder
if she should've let the one who got away go. And she's got a secret—her twins
belong to Adam, her first love, and so does her heart...

**YOU CAN FIND MORE INFORMATION ON UPCOMING HARLEQUIN® TITLES,
FREE EXCERPTS AND MORE AT WWW.HARLEQUIN.COM.**

HSECNM0316

REQUEST YOUR FREE BOOKS!

2 FREE NOVELS PLUS 2 FREE GIFTS!

H HARLEQUIN®

SPECIAL EDITION

Life, Love & Family

YES! Please send me 2 FREE Harlequin® Special Edition novels and my 2 FREE gifts (gifts are worth about $10). After receiving them, if I don't wish to receive any more books, I can return the shipping statement marked "cancel." If I don't cancel, I will receive 6 brand-new novels every month and be billed just $4.74 per book in the U.S. or $5.49 per book in Canada. That's a savings of at least 12% off the cover price! It's quite a bargain! Shipping and handling is just 50¢ per book in the U.S. and 75¢ per book in Canada.* I understand that accepting the 2 free books and gifts places me under no obligation to buy anything. I can always return a shipment and cancel at any time. Even if I never buy another book, the two free books and gifts are mine to keep forever.

235/335 HDN GH3Z

Name _____ (PLEASE PRINT)

Address _____ Apt. #

City _____ State/Prov. _____ Zip/Postal Code

Signature (if under 18, a parent or guardian must sign)

Mail to the **Reader Service:**
IN U.S.A.: P.O. Box 1867, Buffalo, NY 14240-1867
IN CANADA: P.O. Box 609, Fort Erie, Ontario L2A 5X3

Want to try two free books from another line?
Call 1-800-873-8635 or visit www.ReaderService.com.

* Terms and prices subject to change without notice. Prices do not include applicable taxes. Sales tax applicable in N.Y. Canadian residents will be charged applicable taxes. Offer not valid in Quebec. This offer is limited to one order per household. Not valid for current subscribers to Harlequin Special Edition books. All orders subject to credit approval. Credit or debit balances in a customer's account(s) may be offset by any other outstanding balance owed by or to the customer. Please allow 4 to 6 weeks for delivery. Offer available while quantities last.

Your Privacy—The Reader Service is committed to protecting your privacy. Our Privacy Policy is available online at www.ReaderService.com or upon request from the Reader Service.

We make a portion of our mailing list available to reputable third parties that offer products we believe may interest you. If you prefer that we not exchange your name with third parties, or if you wish to clarify or modify your communication preferences, please visit us at www.ReaderService.com/consumerchoice or write to us at Reader Service Preference Service, P.O. Box 9062, Buffalo, NY 14240-9062. Include your complete name and address.

HSE15

SPECIAL EXCERPT FROM

◆ HARLEQUIN®

SPECIAL EDITION

*Obstetrician Avery Wallace treats pregnant patients,
but now she's sporting her own baby bump, thanks to
one passionate night with Dr. Justin Garrett. The good
doctor is eager to put his playboy ways in the past.
But can the daddy-to-be convince Avery to make their
instant family a reality?*

*Read on for a sneak preview of
TWO DOCTORS & A BABY, the latest book in*
Brenda Harlen*'s fan-favorite series,*
THOSE ENGAGING GARRETTS!

"Thank you for tonight," she said as she walked him to
the door. "I was planning on leftovers when I got home—
this was better."

"I thought so, too." He settled his hands on her hips
and drew her toward him.

She put her hands on his chest, determined to hold him
at a distance. "What are you doing?"

"I'm going to kiss you goodbye."

"No, you're not," she said, a slight note of panic in
her voice.

"It's just a kiss, Avery." He held her gaze as his hand
slid up her back to the nape of her neck. "And hardly our
first."

Then he lowered his head slowly, the focused
intensity of those green eyes holding her captive as his
mouth settled on hers. Warm and firm and deliciously

intoxicating. Her own eyes drifted shut as a soft sigh whispered between her lips.

He kept the kiss gentle, patiently coaxing a response. She wanted to resist, but she had no defenses against the masterful seduction of his mouth. She arched against him, opened for him. And the first touch of his tongue to hers was like a lighted match to a candle wick—suddenly she was on fire, burning with desire.

It was like New Year's Eve all over again, but this time she didn't even have the excuse of adrenaline pulsing through her system. This time, it was all about Justin.

Or maybe it was the pregnancy.

Yes, that made sense. Her system was flooded with hormones as a result of the pregnancy, a common side effect of which was increased arousal. It wasn't that she was pathetically weak or even that he was so temptingly irresistible. It wasn't about Justin at all—it was a basic chemical reaction that was overriding her common sense and self-respect. Because even though she knew that he was wrong for her in so many ways, being with him, being in his arms, felt so right.

Don't miss
TWO DOCTORS & A BABY
by Brenda Harlen,
available April 2016 wherever
Harlequin® Special Edition books and ebooks are sold.

www.Harlequin.com

HARLEQUIN®

A *Romance* FOR EVERY MOOD™

JUST CAN'T GET ENOUGH?

Join our social communities
and talk to us online.

You will have access to the latest
news on upcoming titles and special
promotions, but most importantly,
you can talk to other fans about your
favorite Harlequin reads.

Harlequin.com/Community

 Facebook.com/HarlequinBooks

 Twitter.com/HarlequinBooks

Pinterest.com/HarlequinBooks

THE WORLD IS BETTER WITH

Romance

Harlequin has everything from contemporary, passionate and heartwarming to suspenseful and inspirational stories.

Whatever your mood, we have a romance just for you!

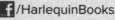